DEFENCE AGAINST TERROR

'I . . . I'm from Costa Verde,' he said, looking curiously at the man driving the van. 'My name is Manuel Frame. I'm a businessman in San Felipe.'

'I'm John Smith. Just call me Hannibal. That's B.A. Baracus.' The driver turned around and forced something like a smile to his face. Manuel Frame gulped. The driver was a burly black man in a tight red T-shirt, overalls, boots, and a cascade of gold chains. His hair was shaved to give him a Mandinka-cut and there were some feathers hanging down from it. Hannibal smiled as he lit a cigar. 'Don't let him charm you like that,' he said. 'The B and A are for Bad Attitude. Now tell us about your problem . . .'

Also available in Target

THE A-TEAM PLOT IT YOURSELF 1:

DEFENCE AGAINST TERROR

William Rotsler

TARGET

A TARGET BOOK
published by
the Paperback Division of
W. H. Allen & Co. PLC

A Target Book
Published in 1985
by the Paperback Division of
W. H. Allen & Co. PLC
44 Hill Street, London W1X 8LB

First published in the United States of America by Wanderer Books
A Division of Simon & Schuster, Inc., 1983
Designed by Stanley S. Drate

Phototypeset by Input Typesetting Ltd, London
Printed and bound in Great Britain by
Anchor Brendon Ltd, Tiptree, Essex

ISBN 0 426 201515

DEFENCE AGAINST TERROR

Ten years ago a crack commando unit was sent to prison by a military court for a crime its members didn't commit. These men promptly escaped from a maximum security stockade to the Los Angeles underground.

Today, still wanted by the government, they survive as soldiers of fortune. If you have a problem and no one else can help . . . and if you can find them . . . maybe you can hire . . . the A-Team.

The man sat nervously in a cafe, frequently turning his head, looking at his watch, licking his lips. He glanced with irritation at the skaters on the sidewalk a few feet away. It was a warm California day, with the sun sparkling on the Pacific a hundred yards away, across the dimpled sand of Venice Beach.

All around him sat men and women, eating an early lunch, laughing, talking, reading. On the wide concrete path in front of the cafe and the stores that faced the sea, there was a steady stream of tourists and natives walking, hurrying, and sauntering back and forth. A large number of them skated, and most of them did it very well. A little distance down the block a dark-skinned man in some kind of arab costume, with a guitar and a grin, skated in graceful curves as he charmed two young girls fresh in from Fond du Lac, Wisconsin.

To the south of the cafe were some shops where luggage, jewelry, trinkets, and souvenirs were sold. A

Turn to page 2.

beautiful blonde woman wearing a headband skated by without seeming to propel herself. Two kids chased each other, darting around the obstacles of people on the concrete road.

The man in the cafe looked at his watch again. 'You shouldn't wear a watch,' someone said, and the man jerked his head around to stare at an old hippie at the next table. He was grey-bearded and unkempt, wearing ancient, patched denims, an embroidered denim jacket, and a T-shirt that indicated: THE MEEK SHALL INHERIT THE EARTH. THE REST OF US WILL GO TO THE STARS.

The man glared from his worn leather cowboy hat to his sandals, then sniffed. 'No, I mean it,' the old hippie said, hitching his metal chair closer with a squeak. 'If you wear a watch you get too tied to time. Relax, man, enjoy. Smell the flowers.'

The man tried to stare the grey-bearded hippie down, but the dishevelled man just smiled. 'Time's a killer, man. You pay too much attention to it and it will *own* you!'

'Señor, kindly mind your own business!'

The hippie just grinned and leaned closer. 'I am. I understand you're looking for the A-Team.'

The man with the accent started, then tried to look into the old face under the leather hat. 'I . . . I was waiting for someone . . . .'

'Your waiting is over,' the man said with a grin. 'Just pay your bill and follow me.'

The hippie sauntered south and laughed at a pair of college girls who had tumbled to the sand bordering the concrete path. One wore a T-shirt which proclaimed that science fiction was for people who couldn't take reality.

In no apparent hurry, the hippie wandered onto a street leading away from the beach, past a building with a mural of the street itself on it. He casually got into a black van parked next to the arches that held the last plaster remnants of the turn-of-the-century attempt to make Venice, California, a replica of Venice, Italy.

The door of the van remained invitingly open, and the nervous man looked up and down the street before he entered it. The door slammed shut, and the van started up and drove off quickly, but at legal speed.

'Tell us more,' the hippie said. The stranger watched with amazement as the hippie stripped off the beard, the leather hat, and a little make-up to become a handsome silver-haired man with a wide grin. 'Go on,' the man said encouragingly.

'I . . . I'm from Costa Verde,' he said, looking curiously at the man driving the van. 'My name is Manuel Frame. I'm a businessman in San Felipe.'

'I'm John Smith. Just call me Hannibal. That's B.A. Baracus.' The driver turned around and forced something like a smile to his face. Manuel Frame gulped. The driver was a burly black man in a tight red T-shirt, overalls, boots, and a cascade of gold chains. His hair was shaved to give him a Mandinka-cut and there were some feathers hanging down from it. Hannibal smiled as he lit a cigar. 'Don't let him charm you like that,' he said. 'The B and A are for Bad Attitude. Now tell us about your problem.'

The nervous man hesitated. 'If this got back to Costa Verde . . . ' Hannibal smiled reassuringly and Manuel Frame went on. 'I'm an importer-exporter. My father was American. I'm almost the only one who can leave the country. If the general found out I was . . . seeing you . . . '

Turn to page 4.

'Hey,' said B.A. 'Is that General Camarillo?' Frame nodded, and B.A. shook his head. 'I hear he's a tough one, Hannibal. Maybe we oughta pass on this one.'

'The general is the brand-new dictator of Costa Verde, isn't he?' Hannibal asked.

'*Si*, but he has been in power long enough to be really . . . How do you say it here? Plugged in? He has the army; the parliament is afraid of him. He . . . he does what he wants.'

'And what do you want us to do?' Hannibal asked.

'Get my daughter out of his palace. They took Nola nine days ago. The secret police—the *Cachiporro*, the Blackjacks—took her.'

'Why?'

'Because she is beautiful and because . . . because the general loves her.'

'And she does not love him?' Hannibal asked.

Frame nodded, looking sad. 'My daughter and I have not been as close as . . . as perhaps we should. I cannot believe she would love such a man. But he believes he can win her, in time.'

'And if he does not?' Hannibal asked softly.

Frame licked his lips. 'Then no one shall have her.'

'Do you know our fee?'

'*Si*, the young woman told me. I . . . I have it with me, at my hotel.'

'It could be a trap, Hannibal, if we go there,' B.A. grumbled.

Hannibal smiled. 'Don't worry. Lynch is chasing his tail in Stockton. Somehow he got the idea I was working stunts on a movie up there.' Lynch was the army officer who had made it his personal vendetta to return each and every one of the A-Team to the stockade.

'We gonna have to fly down there, Hannibal?' B.A. griped.

'He hates to fly,' Hannibal explained to Frame. 'Well, B.A., it would be quicker. It's a long way to Costa Verde.'

'No way, Hannibal. We can drive; we can take the train; we can *walk*, but we don't fly.'

'Well, that's all right, B.A. We can leave you out of this one.' B.A.'s scowl deepened while he took the meandering course through the streets with sharper corners. 'Take Señor Frame back to his car, B.A.' To the exporter, he said, 'We'll be in touch. But meanwhile, give us everything you know about this General Camarillo, about the palace, and about any organized resistance.'

Frame began to talk.

They met at the safe house they were using in Venice, at the corner of Walnut and Carlton Way. 'All right, Triple-A, let's hear what the news services say about General Geraldo Camarillo,' Hannibal said.

Amy Amanda Allen brushed back her long brown hair and looked at her notes. 'Well, he's a real general, not a jumped-up colonel . . . .' She smiled at Hannibal, who had been a colonel, while he waved a smoking cigar in response. 'His politics are mixed, but mostly extreme right wing. No communist influences that anyone can see. He's out to save his country from the communists even if he has to kill it to do that.' She turned a page. 'He has managed to give certain of his relatives rather cushy jobs. He has a Swiss bank account.'

Templeton Peck whistled. 'I just love it when the noble leaders have Swiss bank accounts. It's so . . . engaging.'

Turn to page 6.   5

'Never mind, Face,' Hannibal said. 'What is his psychological profile?'

'A romantic. Very *macho*, very conservative in dress . . . but a killer, too. He'd rescue a kitten from a tree, then probably execute the person who owned the cat for endangering an animal and causing needless government expenditure. He took power in a revolt and is maintaining that power with strong measures. Quite successfully, I might add.'

'All right. Face?'

'Costa Verde's chief exports are coffee, bananas, cocoa, sugar cane, rice, timber, some beans. There's very little real industry, just agricultural products. The per capita income is less than one thousand dollars. The capital is San Felipe; the population is 215,000.'

'Thanks, Face. Amy, does the general have any vices?'

'Outside of kidnapping young women? None to speak of unless you count putting relatives in high places.'

'All right. I think I have a way in. We are going to become a multinational corporation, heavy industry just eager to get in there and develop the country, take advantage of the raw materials and cheap labour. Think he'd go for that?'

Amy nodded. 'He has been trying to get the biggies interested, but to little effect. They're afraid of a counter-revolt.'

Hannibal looked at Face. 'Better get Murdock out of the V.A.'

'Hey, wait a minute!' B.A. growled. 'You planning to *fly* down there? I told you—'

'Now, don't worry, B.A.,' Face said soothingly. 'We're just going to need everyone, that's all.'

'B.A., get our gear together, will you?' Hannibal asked with a smile. B.A. left, glowering.

'What are we going to use this time?' Face asked.

Hannibal grinned and took a drag on his cigar. 'Do you think the old pill-in-the-milk routine will do one more time?'

'I dunno,' Face grimaced. 'Sometimes he gets so . . . so *violent* afterwards.'

'I'll think of something,' Hannibal said. 'We could use a Lear jet, though. And Amy, papers for, um, let's see . . . IPC. International Products Corporation. A Delaware corporation with branches anywhere you can spell. A sign for the jet. Did my business suit come back from the cleaners? Face, you're the vice president in charge of public relations for IPC. I'm, oh, John Hannibal, executive V.P. of acquisitions and development. Amy, get off a series of cables to the good general advising him of our arrival. Ask him to prepare some sort of report on available land with sea access, local weather conditions, labour pool, and . . . well, anything you think up.' Hannibal grinned and waved his cigar. 'I just love it when a plan starts to come together.'

Amy and Templeton Peck looked at each other and rolled their eyes.

To see Murdock 'fly', turn to page 8.
To see Murdock in a different role, turn to page 9.   7

From page 7.

Templeton Peck smoothed down his false moustache, straightened his white doctor's coat, and pinned on the ID badge: L. GRAY, M.D. Face had found it advantageous to 'acquire' a number of such badges over the years since they had broken out of the stockade. He picked up his clipboard and left the linen room where he had acquired the jacket.

The halls of the Veterans Administration Hospital were painted a glossy neutral colour and seemed endless. But Face knew exactly where 'Howling Mad' Murdock lived—or rather, was kept. It was in that section unofficially reserved for the permanently insane, but relatively harmless, inmates.

As he approached Murdock's room he saw a white flutter of nurses—both male and female—and heard loud squawks over the nervous chatter. Face shouldered his way through the door and saw that two big muscular attendants were trying to get Murdock off the ceiling. The former Vietnam combat pilot was just out of their reach. He had glued fragments of Velcro to the ceiling and to his shoes, and he wore Velcro mittens. He hopped around, moving on to the next spot as his weight began to pull him free.

'I'll get him down,' Face said with authority. 'You Murdock! This is an order! Come down at once!'

'Yes, sir,' Murdock said and did a somersault in the air. He landed on his feet and saluted. 'Captain Murdock reporting, sir!'

Face smiled as he led Murdock out of his room. 'Let's go to my office and discuss this incident.'

To see if Hannibal Smith can keep his cool, turn to page 10.
It might be the spider inviting the fly into his web
on page 11.

From page 7.

The nurse carefully crept into Murdock's room, looking around cautiously. It was in its usual confusion: photographs on the walls of Charles Lindbergh, Steve Canyon, Smilin' Jack, Baron von Richthofen, Jimmy Allen, and the Black Sheep Squadron's commander, 'Pappy' Boyington. In one corner, up on a pile of chairs, was the six-foot nest he had built last month. It still contained four plastic eggs. On one wall were crayon drawings of great complexity: Charlemagne Opening a Fast-food Restaurant . . . Napoleon at Malibu . . . Emily Brontë at the Supermarket . . . Plato Versus Muhammad Ali at the Garden . . . Lou Costello Invents the Double Take.

'Mister Murdock?' No response. She edged in closer. There was a pile of cardboard boxes painted and cut to look roughly like the New York skyline. 'Captain Murdock?'

'Kong!' a voice thundered. Murdock, dressed in pyjamas, with hundreds of snips of typewriter ribbon taped to his clothes, came up from the cardboard skyline and tried to climb the Empire State Building. It didn't work. From his subsequent reclining position on the floor he said in a perfectly calm voice, 'What is it, Nurse Nightingale?'

'There's . . . uh . . . there's a relative of yours out here, a Mister Peck? He has a day-furlough pass for you. You be good out there now, you hear?'

Murdock rose with dignity. 'I am *always* good, but sometimes I'm better,' he intoned.

The action really gets going on page 12.

Murdock grinned at the Lear jet but then frowned at the uniform that was handed to him. 'I wore a uniform once,' he grumbled. 'I was a captain.'

'We know,' Face said gently. 'But if you wear this one, we'll let you fly that plane.'

Murdock let out an eagle's cry and reached for the uniform. He examined the badge over the right pocket. 'Charles Lang, Chief Pilot, IPC.' He looked at Face. 'I, Pilot Captain?'

As Face explained about International Products, Hannibal arrived in the van with Amy, driven by B.A., who glowered meanly at the jet. 'I knew it,' he grumbled. 'I knew it.'

'Oh, that's all right,' Hannibal said. 'You don't have to go. You can stay here and answer the phones in case they check on us. You can be a vice president or something.'

'I ain't gonna fly.'

'No one asked you. Would you help Face get the gear out of the van? Amy, go aboard. Murdock, warm it up.' He looked at his watch, then at Face. 'Any time now.' Face nodded and kept close to B.A. Baracus.

'Why are you on my heels, fool?' B.A. grumbled. 'You'd think . . . ' He suddenly got a strange expression on his face, gulped, stared, and fell. Face caught him neatly, and Hannibal picked up his ankles.

As they hauled him aboard Hannibal said, 'I'm glad it didn't work when he was driving.' They rolled him into the jet. Within ten minutes they were airborne.

The A-Team goes to meet the bad guys on page 13.
B.A. finds himself where he doesn't want to be on page 14.

10

'You're looking a little strange, B.A.,' Hannibal said as they approached Santa Monica Airport.

'I'm okay,' B.A. said, but he was sweating. *The street seems a little blurry but I'll make it,* he thought. *It must be that fever I caught in Nam coming back. Hannibal said I may have these little seizures from time to time.*

They pulled the black van up to the Lear jet in a way that blocked the view of anyone watching and began transferring their gear. Templeton Peck explained how he had acquired the executive jet by a little blarney, a receptive female desk clerk, and forged documents from a large corporation.

Hannibal looked at his watch, then caught Face's eye and nodded. They moved closer to the muscular B.A., who was saying goodbye to Amy. 'I don't like to fly, and flying with that crazy man is my idea of suicide, so . . . ' He stopped, blinked his eyes, swayed, and fell over backwards. Amy screeched, but Face and Hannibal caught him.

Hannibal smiled at Amy as they lifted Baracus through the narrow jet door. 'Don't worry. His fever will be over about the time we land.'

'Off we go . . . into the wild blue yonder, flying high, into the sky!' Murdock sang over the intercom as he flew the sleek jet off the runway.

'Did you file a flight plan?' Face asked.

'Of *course*,' Murdock answered. 'You think I want to do things *illegally*?'

'You don't have a licence,' Face reminded him, but Murdock just grinned.

Hannibal plays a bluff on page 15.
Deep trouble begins for the A-Team on page 16.

'Oh, it's a beauty,' Amy exclaimed, looking at the sleek Lear jet on the field at Van Nuys Airport. 'I see B.A. got the sign on it.' Across the sides of the white jet were the letters IPC and the world and wreath symbol which Hannibal had picked from a typographer's book.

They all looked very businesslike in their suits as they pulled up. Murdock, in the kind of anonymous uniform companies sometimes use, stuck his head out the window. 'Everything's ready, Colonel!'

'Where's B.A.?' Amy asked. Hannibal just grinned and directed her in through the small hatch, and grinned wider as she yelped, 'He's dead!'

'No, he's just sleeping,' Hannibal said. 'He went to bed about three this morning and I offered him a glass of warm milk to help him sleep.'

'Oh, the old pill-in-the-milk gag, huh?' Face said as they started to taxi. 'But isn't he going to be, um, cross when he wakes up?'

'I'll tell him I knew he wanted to be along for the fun and wouldn't want to miss it,' Hannibal said, buckling up.

'And you couldn't wake him, so . . . ' Amy shrugged. 'Sometime you guys are going to get stomped by B.A.' She smiled sweetly. 'And I wouldn't blame him.'

 Rush on to page 17.

The airport at San Felipe was not exactly Los Angeles International. There was a military field past a fence, where slightly obsolete jet fighters sat in hangars, a gift of the United States. The moustached men wearing dark glasses who met Hannibal's jet were also military, with an abundance of medals on their uniforms.

Hannibal stepped down from the plane in impeccable dress, followed by a smiling Templeton Peck and a quietly efficient secretary, introduced as Ms Armbruster. They were taken through customs at a walk, without even a pretence of inspection, just as Hannibal had guessed.

They were put into a limousine, which, by the sound of the door, was bulletproof. Followed by a truck with a man at the .50-calibre machine gun and a load of immaculate troops, and preceded by a limo full of officers and several motorcycles, they made a swift entry into the city and direct to the presidential palace.

'Señor Hannibal, this way,' an officer said with a smile as they got out. Hannibal paused to look around at the square in front of the palace. Two tanks flanked the palace and he could see guards on the roofs of buildings all around the square.

'We're not trying a frontal attack, that's for sure,' Face muttered to Hannibal.

'I never thought we would,' Hannibal answered.

They went up the steps and into the cool building past guards carrying automatic weapons.

Hannibal tries bribery on page 18.
B.A. takes on an air force on page 19.

While Hannibal, Face and Amy were being met at the San Felipe Airport by a group of officers wearing what seemed like an unusual number of ribbons and medals, B.A. Baracus was coming to in the rear of the Lear jet. He glared at the recognizable curved surfaces around him and got to his feet in a flurry of anger. He stomped through the small jet and grabbed Murdock by the neck.

'What you doing, fool? You ain't takin' off with me on board!'

'*Arrk!*' Murdock gurgled. He waved his hands at the windows and B.A. looked out.

'This ain't Santa Monica!'

Murdock pried B.A.'s fingers from his throat. 'It's San *Felipe*, B.A.! You had a hit of that fever of yours. Hannibal didn't want to leave you behind, unconscious, for just anyone to find!' He smiled reassuringly at the tough black man. 'So we brought you along. Hannibal said you can go back by train, okay?'

B.A. glared at the scenery, then at Murdock. 'All right, man. But I ain't flyin' back—especially with *you*! You're crazy!'

'Of course, I'm crazy. Who said I wasn't? But being crazy doesn't mean I can't fly, now does it?'

'You fly, fool, but you fly *crazy*!'

Murdock smiled and spoke in a French accent. 'Monsieur, I am zee best crazy flyer, and *all* flyers are a wee bit mad, no?'

'Shut up,' B.A. growled. 'What're we supposed to do now?'

'Ahh, zee plans!' Murdock exclaimed. 'Now—zee plans!'

B.A. gets an impossible task on page 20.
14 *Hannibal sets a trap on page 21.*

There were several uniformed officers awaiting them at San Felipe Airport. Hannibal could see that the far end of the field was the military part of Costa Verde's small air force. Hannibal stepped down from the jet with a smile and an extended hand. He was saluted by a colonel who then shook his hand. Hannibal introduced Face as Templeton Peck, his executive assistant, and Amy as Ms Sylvia Milton, his secretary. They had all agreed that Amy should keep out of the limelight as an active member of the A-Team since she had an above-ground job as a reporter, a position that gave them some advantages, and she was a contact for people trying to hire the A-Team.

B.A. Baracus melted into the background by staying inside the plane, but Murdock was introduced with special emphasis as IPC Head Pilot Charles Lang of International Aerospace, an IPC subsidiary. 'He will inspect and evaluate your aircraft inventory, and we will give you his recommendations for upgrading your air defences,' Hannibal said with a wide, confident smile.

B.A. smiled a mean smile inside the Lear jet. 'Crazy fool will probably recommend fifty-foot paper planes,' he grumbled.

'Take me to your leader,' Hannibal said and grinned. 'Ah, Sylvia, smell that! The tropics! Romance!'

Sylvia smiled thinly, smelling rotting vegetation, jet fuel, smoke, and a few other odours she didn't care to identify. 'Yes, sir!' she said agreeably.

They got into a limousine, which Hannibal recognized as being bulletproof, and were driven to the presidential palace.

Hannibal pulls a fast one on page 22.
Greed raises its ugly head on page 23.

From page 11.

During the plane ride to the small Central American country, Hannibal briefed the team on several alternate plans. 'I will have to do it by feel, so pick up on my hints and go along. They are really all variations on one plan.'

'Greed,' Amy said and Hannibal nodded.

'Costa Verde needs trade, but big investors are wary of places with a lot of revolts and abrupt changes of government. So we are going to be the only game in town,' Hannibal explained.

'We hope,' said Templeton Peck with a weak smile.

Hannibal beamed when he saw the military honour guard awaiting them at the airport. 'Your telegrams prepared things well,' he said to Amy.

Murdock swung the plane around to let his passengers out right in front of the officers and honour guard. Hannibal smiled widely as he came down the steps and into the hot sunlight. 'Good afternoon, gentlemen,' he began.

The colonel in charge said, 'This is all of you?'

'Yes, but we are capable of—'

'Seize them!' the colonel commanded, and suddenly Hannibal saw the muzzles of a lot of guns.

'There's some mistake, Colonel. We're here to—'

'I know what you are here to do, you charlatan! Take them to San Pietro!'

San Pietro was a prison built in the seventeenth century. A lot of people went in, rumour had it, but few came out.

Captured! Turn to page 24.

 Prison! Turn to page 25.

From page 12.

It was a long flight, and Hannibal had time to outline several variations on his main plan. 'Watch me for clues,' he said as they circled for a landing at San Felipe.

No one met them, but customs was as thorough as Hannibal expected them to be, which wasn't thorough enough to detect certain objects hidden in their luggage. 'You're certain the telegrams got here?' Hannibal asked Amy, who nodded.

The customs people waved them on. Since the country had so few tourists, they didn't want to offend anyone who might want to spread American dollars around.

'Hotel Nacional,' Hannibal said as they crammed into a taxi. When Amy commented that hotel information hadn't been in the briefing, Hannibal just smiled. 'There's *always* a Hotel Nacional in every city south of Texas.' He lit a cigar, which Amy promptly grabbed and threw out of the crowded taxi.

After they had checked into their rooms, Hannibal had Amy call the president's office. She reported to Hannibal, 'They are expecting you at ten tomorrow morning. I got the feeling they were playing it cool, trying not to appear overeager.'

'Good,' Hannibal said. 'That means they are trying not to blow the deal. Come on, B.A., you and I are going scouting.'

B.A. just nodded, as if night scouting was the usual thing tourists did.

Hannibal's big con starts on page 26.
The general thinks it over on page 28.

From page 13.

General Geraldo Camarillo was a stocky man, moustached and bemedaled. He stood behind a massive desk in the immense presidential office awaiting them. Hannibal thought it done rather well: he didn't have to rise as they entered, yet met them with proper courtesies, on his own turf, with all the symbols of power around him.

After the introductions had been made, General Camarillo sat down and gestured for them to sit in high-backed chairs before the desk. 'And now, what can the Republic of Costa Verde do for you, señor?'

Hannibal stuck out his hand and Amy put a folder into it. Without looking at it, Hannibal said, 'General, may I excuse my associates?'

'Of course,' General Camarillo said smoothly. When the door had closed, Hannibal was offered a cigar, which he lit and blew out a cloud of smoke.

'Now,' Hannibal said, 'let me tell you how to become rich.' He grinned. '*Really* rich. And your country, too, of course.'

'Of course,' the general smiled.

Templeton Peck smiled at the guards outside the office. 'Which way to the living quarters? I believe we are to be guests here.'

'I will show you,' a young lieutenant said, saluting. 'Your luggage has already been sent up.' He bowed and kissed Amy's hand. 'Lieutenant Mendoza, señorita.'

 The danger increases on page 27.

From page 13.

Murdock refueled the jet and positioned it for a swift take-off while B.A. got into overalls and hid his Mandinka-cut hair under a fatigue cap. He slipped around the gasoline truck and disappeared in the direction of the military field.

There was a high fence separating the civilian field from the military, but B.A. solved that problem by jumping on a passing truck and climbing to the canvas top. Then he jumped from there to the ground on the other side, rolling to a motionless stop beneath a parked scout plane.

When he thought no one was looking, he moved into a stack of discarded crates. He carefully noted the position of each jet on the field, the guard posts, and the lights. He planned his approach carefully, then curled up to sleep, awaiting darkness.

The fever seemed to have passed and that made him feel better. It made him feel vulnerable to think that something so small as a virus or bug or whatever it was could knock down a man as big and strong as he was. *Well,* he thought, *here I am in some faraway banana republic and it will be a long ride home on the train, but there is one thing certain—they ain't getting me on that plane!*

No sir, he thought as he curled up. *No way.*

The general is bribed on page 30.
Hannibal's plans move along on page 31.

From page 14.

Murdock looked very serious. 'You have the signal honour, Sergeant Baracus, of immobilizing the Costa Verde Air Force.'

'Say what?'

'It's a small air force, B.A., hardly worth mentioning. A dozen fighters, maybe fifteen. There's only about nine here. The rest are on the other side of the country at their *other* military airport. See over there. That's the military part of this place. You go over there and do something subtle. Block their fuel lines, foul up their electrical system, anything to delay them an hour. By that time we will be off into the wild blue yonder, safe as bugs in a rug.' He shivered and stuck his tongue out. 'Ugh! Bugs in a rug! Uuuug-*lee!*'

'Listen, fool,' B.A. said, grabbing the front of Murdock's IPC uniform. 'You want me to waste an *air force?*'

'Uh, well, not me, B.A. Hannibal wants it. Look, do you mind? I want to look neat. I'm the head pilot for IPC, see? Look at that? See that badge? Head pilots are neat.'

B.A. released him, glowering. 'Well, if Hannibal wants it. It's part of the plan, huh?'

'Yes sir, you bet, an important part. Without it this whole deal is *kaput*, over, concluded, doomed, extinct, made obsolete—got it?'

B.A. looked hard at Murdock, then he went to work to gather the necessary tools and formulate a plan.

General Geraldo Camarillo was a small, thin, slight man, lithe as a whip, with a mean, ferretlike face. *I don't like him*, Hannibal thought as he smiled and extended his hand. 'General,' he said enthusiastically. 'At last! I'm John Hannibal, executive vice president. This is Templeton Peck and my secretary, Ms Fergenschneider.'

'Welcome to Costa Verde, señor,' the general said. 'Would you like a drink? Coffee?' When Hannibal refused, the general spread his hands. 'Ah, you impatient *Americanos*. Business, business, business, always business!'

'That's how we get things done, General. Mister Peck, where is our next destination?'

'Mexico City, sir. The oil deal?'

'Yes, of course. General, I'm very sorry that we can give you only a certain amount of our time on this. I'm certain you will understand. You are a busy man, too, what with the guerrillas and all.'

The general flushed angrily. 'That problem is almost over, Señor Hannibal.'

'I'm sure it is, General. You'll understand that the follow-up work will be done by my subordinates, once you and I . . . ' Hannibal gave a discreet cough. ' . . . have reached a satisfactory agreement on general principles. My company will only deal with the top man, one who is firmly in control and likely to be in power for a long time. You understand, of course.'

'Of course,' the general said and smiled knowingly.

The A-Team shows its courage on page 32.
The A-Team starts night action on page 33.   21

From page 15.

General Geraldo Camarillo looked older than his fifty years, grey-haired and distinguished, like a retired Mafia don. He had the look of power and the extra look of a man ready to defend it with any means available.

'General, we at International Products are here to bring you into the twentieth century,' Hannibal said. He ignored the dictator's frown. 'Our aerospace division has come up with just the fighter you need—versatile, relatively inexpensive, capable of landing on short fields to work closely with troops . . . .' He paused significantly and the general caught on.

'Anti-guerrilla?' the general asked.

'Precisely. It can strafe, drop napalm, bombs, whatever you want, precisely controlled from the ground by on-the-spot commanders.'

General Camarillo sat back in his ornate gold chair. 'And what will this cost us, this modern weapons system?' He looked suspicious, yet greedy, too.

Hannibal smiled slyly. 'We have an offer, General, one I think you can't refuse. The plane is called the Smasher, and it is so new that the prototypes are just coming off the assembly line. We need promotional film, footage under actual combat conditions, if you know what I mean. We would give you six aircraft for four months of use with trained ground crews. You pay for ammunition and so forth. If you like, you buy . . . and we get the promotional material we need for worldwide sales. Our chief pilot, Mister Lang, will need to evaluate your present planes and facilities.'

'Señor, I think we have a deal,' General Camarillo said.

Murdock heads for trouble on page 34.
Amy prepares for trouble on page 35.

From page 15.

'Howdy, General,' Murdock said, sticking out his hand to the paunchy dictator. 'I'm Lang, Charles Lang? See, it's on my badge here? Charles Lang, Head Pilot, IPC. That means there is no one better than me . . . or is it I?' He looked to Hannibal for confirmation, but the silver-haired A-Team commander moved in smoothly.

'The best, that's our Charlie,' Hannibal said and smiled. 'Look, General, I'm afraid I don't have much time. You know how we American businessmen are—rush, rush, rush. I have to be in . . . ' He looked to Amy, who spoke up at once.

'Caracas, Venezuela, sir. The petroleum deal with Exxon.'

'Oh. I thought it was Mobil.'

'That's next month, sir, in New York.'

'Of course, of course. Glad you're around, Ms Milton. You see, General Camarillo, how busy I am? The *final* negotiations will be finalized by the final negotiators, of course. We are just here to open discussion and define the parameters of the operation.'

'I see,' the general said slowly. 'But you have the power to . . . make promises?'

'Of course, that's my job,' Hannibal said. 'This is a complex issue but we need your input. We need a trial zone for our new Smasher line of anti-guerrilla fighters, a site for the gasohol plant—and that's budgeted at $100 million, by the way—and a few other odds and ends. With your sugar cane and your ready supply of guerrillas we can satisfy both needs in no time, General.'

Murdock sends B.A. to risk his life on page 36.
Hannibal gets the A-Team ready for the final act on page 37.

23

From page 16.

Three soldiers with rifles entered the Lear jet, crowding it with menace. One of the soldiers prodded awake B.A. Baracus, who looked around him with a disgusted and grumpy expression. The other two soldiers went into the pilot's compartment.

'Hey, I'm just a hired plane jockey,' Murdock said. 'I never saw those guys before this morning, honest!' He smiled disarmingly, but no one bought it. They herded Murdock and B.A. out at gunpoint. However, the other soldiers had already left in a cloud of dust, with Hannibal, Face, and Amy as their prisoners.

The soldiers left behind yelled, but no one paid them any attention. Sullenly, they prodded Murdock and the big black ex-sergeant with their rifles and started to walk back toward town. Suddenly, in a casual voice, B.A. started to defame the ancestry, eating habits, and personal hygiene of the guards, much to Murdock's surprise and nervousness.

'B.A., be careful. These birds may have itchy trigger fingers.'

'Shut up, fool. Can't you see they don't understand English? American, either. See that patch of jungle up there? When he gets up there, get ready.'

'B.A., please. My bulletproofing from Nam may have worn off. Don't try anything like that. Maybe we can talk our way out of this.' He saw the look on B.A.'s face and gulped. 'Oh, dear . . . ' he sighed.

B.A. moved like a hurricane, leaving two guards sprawled in the dust.

B.A. and Murdock struggle in the jungle on page 38.

24 *Hannibal plans an escape on page 39.*

From page 16.

The entire A-Team was thrown into a single cell, despite Murdock's plea that he was just a hired pilot who didn't even *know* these people. He found a tin cup and at once was rattling it back and forth on the bars. 'You dirty rats! You dirty rats!' He stopped and looked at Face. 'What did Jimmy say then?'

'He didn't even say that. Sit down, Murdock.'

'Well, here we are together,' said Hannibal with a smile.

'You know, Hannibal, sometimes I could punch you out for being cheerful,' B.A. growled. But that didn't deter Hannibal.

'Do we have them where we want them or do we have them where we want them?' Hannibal asked and grinned.

B.A. looked at Murdock, then asked Hannibal, 'Can people catch crazy?'

'Don't ask me. This is my first time going through insanity.'

'What's your plan?' Amy asked.

'I'm still working on it,' he replied.

'That means he doesn't have one,' Face explained.

Hannibal still didn't have one when the soldiers came to take them out of the cell at twilight. Under heavy guard they were transported to a concrete athletic arena and herded onto the patchy grass and sand in the centre of the floodlit stadium.

In a cluster in the seats the team could make out a small, uniformed group of men and one woman. 'Hannibal, isn't that Nola Frame?' Amy whispered.

'Quiet,' Hannibal ordered. 'Don't look scared. Providing you are, of course,' he added.

'Are you *kidding*?' Amy asked.

The A-Team is in the arena of death on page 40.
The A-Team is pitted against the knife fighters on page 41. 25

From page 17.

Hannibal and B.A. walked along the quiet streets as evening fell. There was some laughter and guitar music from a cafe, some drunken song from a cantina. The presidential palace was a formidable structure, as big as the White House, but with only one entrance on each side. It seemed well guarded as they circled it in the bushes.

'Well, Hannibal? Shall I steal a tank?'

'No, come on, B.A. I've got to think about this. This may be the place for guile and subterfuge.'

'For what?'

'Sneaky stuff.'

At precisely ten the next morning, Mr John Hannibal and staff presented themselves to El Presidente General Camarillo's personal secretary. He smiled thinly and escorted them into the dictator's office.

Hannibal provided the general with the introductions: 'Mister Peck, my personal assistant and public relations officer . . . Mister Lang, our chief pilot in the aerospace division . . . Mister Baracus, security . . . and, of course, Ms Freiganburger, my secretary.'

The general was an immensely gross man, whose natural expression was a flat stare and a scowl. He and B.A. scowled at each other before the general turned to Hannibal. 'Señor, we are honoured. I have made inquiries regarding your company but regrettably my ambassador at the United Nations is having difficulty finding your corporate headquarters.'

Hannibal smiled easily. 'We just merged with General Astronautics and Gilliland Oil.' He coughed uncomfortably. 'There is something of a revolt going on in the boardroom, General. You understand. Each company wants *its* name to be dominant. But IPC *will* win out in the end. Now, as to the reason we are here.'

Amy took meaningless notes as Hannibal snowed the general about the investments that IPC was prepared to make in the future of Costa Verde. The gasohol plant alone would cost over $100 million, which would make alcohol from sugar cane and mix it with Mexican oil. Then there was the military option, using Costa Verde as a proving ground for the prototype of the new Skysword class air-support fighter-bomber. Mixed in with this were sly references to the general about forming a private corporation to buy and lease land and other services to IPC. General Camarillo bit.

After a few well-placed comments by Amy, the general insisted on giving them a tour of the palace. Back in the hotel they compared notes about where they thought Nola Frame might be hidden. 'The suite with the two soldiers, right?' Face said.

'There isn't a tower to be sealed up in,' Murdock said, 'so I guess the suite, too.'

'Fool,' muttered B.A. 'But how do we get in?'

'I have a plan,' Hannibal said.

'Amy,' Face said, 'before long you will notice a certain gleam in his eye. Gleam One means the plan will work. Gleam Two means that it won't work, but it could. Gleam Three means it'll never work, but with faith, wisdom, luck, and courage, it *might* work.'

'And this gleam was?'

Face held up three fingers.

The A-Team goes after the target on page 66.

Hannibal and B.A. returned from their scout of the palace with the report that everything seemed pretty well guarded. But at ten the next morning they found the subject of their expedition walking down the hall as they walked up to the desk of the president's secretary.

Face said quickly, 'The lavatory, *por favor*?' The secretary pointed down the corridor. Fortunately, it was in the same direction that Nola Frame was walking, followed by a *dueña* and two armed guards. Face excused himself and followed her. Hannibal led the rest of the group into the president's office.

General Camarillo was younger than his pictures had indicated. He was handsome and cynical. After introductions he said, 'And I suppose the great IPC has come here to dispense largesse among the poor peasants?'

'Not exactly,' Hannibal said and smiled. 'I thought we might make the rich richer.'

A look of surprise showed on the dictator's face. 'Do you have anyone particularly in mind?'

'You, of course. And perhaps certain key members of your *junta*. The others will merely become wealthy.'

'And how shall that come to pass?' General Camarillo asked. Hannibal detected a certain breathlessness in the general which he exploited ruthlessly in the next half hour. Long-term loans, corporate investments, key site acquisition for gasohol processing plants, a military commitment by the US government, a long-term naval base on generous terms, and many other propositions were offered. 'I must think on this,' the general said, and Hannibal nodded wisely.

---

28   *The A-Team makes their move on page 42.*

From page 18.

Hannibal and General Camarillo shook hands in his plush office. There had only been a minimum of haggling. Both knew the agreement could be terminated by the general at any time, even after International Products had built the $100 million plant for turning the abundant sugar cane and other agricultural products into alcohol, which would then be mixed with gasoline to make gasohol—enough to give OPEC a serious run for their money.

The general knew he could nationalize the company's assets, but he just didn't know there was no company. However, nationalizing wouldn't help him personally; it would be better to stick with this obviously ambitious and avaricious vice president. There was enough to go around.

'Now, General, I'd like to freshen up, then dine, perhaps. Tomorrow we can see some of the possible sites,' Hannibal said and smiled.

'Of course,' the general said and pressed a button.

In Hannibal's room a few minutes later, aware that it might be bugged, Face, Amy, and Hannibal exchanged messages on paper while making casual remarks or dictating orders to the fictitious home office on the progress of negotiations.

SECTION OF LIVING QUARTERS CLOSED OFF, Face wrote. MANY GUARDS.

AMY—YOUR JOB—GET IN, RECON, AND GET OUT! Hannibal wrote.

Amy nodded and shrugged. Face took the paper and scribbled: USE YOUR CONSIDERABLE CHARMS. EITHER THAT OR PUNCH OUT THE GUARDS.

She punched him in the arm.

Amy tries her wiles on page 43.
There's no turning back after page 44.

29

From page 19.

General Geraldo Camarillo was a handsome man, with a dapper moustache and an impeccably tailored uniform covered with medals. His office was large, and his desk was flanked by both the national flag and his own personal flag. A huge portrait of himself on horseback was on the wall, although Amy had said his file indicated that he hated horses.

Images, thought Hannibal as he shook hands. 'Please,' the general said, indicating chairs. 'I pride myself on knowing how to deal with you vigorous Americans,' he said with a touch of pomposity. 'So shall we get directly to the point?'

'Excellent, General, but first, may we talk in private?'

The dictator gave him a searching look, then with a wave of his hand dismissed everyone. He watched Amy exit with an appraising look, then turned to Hannibal. 'You look for a "deal", as I believe you *Americanos* call it?'

Hannibal smiled his alligator smile. 'You *do* understand how we work, don't you? Well, here it is' For an hour Hannibal spelled out an elaborate plan, talking high finance, corporate investments, long-term loans from eastern banks, and so on, but what Camarillo seemed to enjoy and understand best was the part about the $1.4 million up front and the steady payments into his Swiss account. That IPC knew about the account didn't seem to bother him. They shook hands, smiled, and declared agreement. 'Based on an examination of the sites and verification of certain understandings, of course,' Hannibal said.

'And a million four,' added the general.

30   *The A-Team is committed on page 45.*

The handsome, rather dashing general met his guests in the grand ballroom, and after some polite talk he took Hannibal into his office for more private conversation. This left Face and Amy to wander around the palace.

'Hannibal will snow him with his Big Business Talk Number Four and play on his greed,' Face said, 'and we, my dear, go exploring.'

But they discovered that certain areas of the palace were off limits to them. Armed guards politely blocked their way, but they saw an old woman going through a guarded door, carrying laundry. 'Women's things,' Amy whispered.

They went to their rooms, made certain arrangements, and took separate paths at different times to enlarge their knowledge of the big building.

Hannibal joined them, smiling and smoking a big Havana cigar. He cupped his hand to his ear, and Face said, 'I couldn't find any eavesdropping bugs.'

'Good. Well, he bit. Now what have you found out?'

The A-Team starts the dangerous part on page 45.

From page 21.

At that point Hannibal feigned a certain weariness and suggested they begin the real negotiations in the morning. They were shown to their adjoining rooms. Amy took an evening walk around the palace and its gardens, escorted by a suave Captain Mendoza, who was only too eager to show the naive American woman the lush palace.

When she returned and had got rid of Mendoza—no easy task—Amy went into Hannibal's room. 'I think I know where Nola *might* be. There are two guards stationed at a suite, and Mendoza said there was a special guest in there. He seemed uncomfortable, so I didn't pursue it.'

'Good work, Triple-A,' Face said and grinned.

'I wonder how B.A. and Murdock are doing?' Hannibal wondered.

At that moment Murdock was reading a comic book, *Mighty Hunk Versus Dinosoid, the Creature from Time.* He read the words aloud, using various voices: Howard Cosell for Dinosoid, Jimmy Stewart for Electro Boy, the fastest kid in the world, and Marlene Dietrich for Bobby Sue Evil, the villainess. For the Mighty Hunk he did a rather poor but enthusiastic Ronald Reagan and for Maureen Lucas, he used the voice of Joan Rivers.

Meanwhile, B.A. Baracus was risking his life going over a guarded fence.

32   *They find their quarry on page 56.*

Pleading a certain amount of weariness, Hannibal left General Camarillo and was escorted to the three-room suite on the second floor, which had been made ready for them. It was left to Face and Amy to go on an early evening stroll and locate likely locations where Nola Frame might be.

Hannibal unpacked their equipment from the suitcase linings and handles and from the base of Amy's secretarial typewriter. Hannibal sighed as he looked at the nearly brand-new business suits he had brought. They would all be left behind, along with Amy's dresses and Face's clothes. But they had to put the proper things in the luggage in case they were searched.

Hannibal methodically began to remove gear from his shaving brush handle, from the toothpaste tube, and from within a bar of soap. Some pills labelled as vitamins were mashed and mixed together in a tooth glass to make an explosive. A walking cane was the barrel and chamber of a single-shot rifle; the trigger mechanism was taken from a jar of Amy's cold cream.

Then Hannibal took out their tight-fitting black clothes and lay down to rest. Twenty minutes later Amy and Templeton Peck gave their report, narrowing the likely locations down to the dungeons below the palace and a suite in the east wing, which was the only one guarded.

'Suit up,' Hannibal said. 'We'll go along the ledge out there to that wing. The clock is running.'

Turn to page 66.

General Camarillo ordered two officers to escort Murdock—in his Charles Lang disguise—to the military field. En route Murdock claimed he had to get his chief mechanic, Mister Baracus. 'He's a little eccentric,' Murdock said, smiling and tapping his temple, 'but he is really an excellent mechanic. His mother dresses him funny, but . . . ' Murdock shrugged. 'You have to tolerate eccentrics, you know, especially when they are the best there is.'

Murdock smiled benignly as the two Latin officers nodded in bewildered agreement. They stared at B.A.'s one hundred gold necklaces, seven earrings, fourteen ankle chains, and ten rings. But they didn't say anything to the scowling, bearded man as he climbed into the jeep.

'Mister Hannibal wants you to check out the condition of the aircraft,' Murdock said. 'I shall take a test flight in their best airplane, which you shall select.'

B.A. nodded. He knew what that meant. The 'best' plane was the one most fully armed, and his 'check out' was to disable the rest of them.

They drove into the military half of the airport, and Murdock smiled. So far it was duck soup. 'Ever have duck soup?' he asked the officer on his right. 'Is it easy or what?'

Hannibal sets up the general on page 46.
Murdock starts the party rolling from three miles up on page 47.

From page 22.

Hannibal watched Murdock swagger off and half smiled at his cocky manner. Murdock was enjoying his new status as head pilot for a huge international corporation, even if the company was phony.

Hannibal turned to General Camarillo and asked permission to allow his assistants to go to their rooms. 'We have to be in Mexico City quite soon, and there is much to be prepared.' He smiled apologetically. 'IPC has ongoing negotiations all over the world, including one, I might add, with the second largest oil company.' He smiled reassuringly at the general. 'You might buy stock now, General Camarillo, as the merger is certain to push the price up.'

Amy and Face slipped out quietly and were shown to their rooms. 'Now to find where Nola Frame is kept,' Amy said.

'While Hannibal dazzles the little general with dreams of wealth and glory,' Face said and grinned. He looked at his watch. 'Dark in three hours.'

'I'll get dressed,' Amy said and went to her room, where she pulled out a beautiful evening gown from one of Rodeo Drive's best fashion houses, an expensive item bought with Manuel Frame's advance. 'I hope I don't have to leave this behind,' she sighed.

The rescuers go to work on page 48.

Murdock was sent off with an escort of three colonels to inspect the Costa Verde Air Force on its single military field. 'My first recommendation, gentlemen,' Murdock said in his best character-actor's voice, 'is that you get yourself another field. You are vulnerable here. Two bombs, one on each runway, and you couldn't fly.'

'We know that, señor. Another field in the mountains is half completed. The previous regime relied more on ground troops and tanks to maintain control,' explained one of the colonels.

'He who controls the air controls the soil,' Murdock said pompously. 'This is your entire inventory of planes?'

'*Si.* Nine. Two are in repair facilities. One crashed last month. The pilot has been executed.'

Murdock looked at him in amazement. 'You shot the pilot?'

'It keeps the others from committing errors. He shouldn't have bailed out of his plane. We might have been able to salvage it. After all, it was nearly 10 per cent of our entire air fleet.'

Murdock looked at B.A., who they had picked up at the Lear jet en route. 'Mister Baracus, would you see to the mechanical status?' As B.A. moved away, attracting stares of disbelief from the colonels, Murdock said, 'Unusual-looking man, I realize, but he's absolutely top notch. Crazy as a loon, however.' At their startled looks he shrugged. 'He won't fly. Scared to death. Look at him. You'd think nothing would scare him, correct? We have to take him places in chains half the time. Yes, totally insane on that one subject. Otherwise,' Murdock said and grinned, 'a barrel of laughs.'

 The A-Team gets going on the rescue work on page 48.

From page 23.

Things began to happen rather quickly.

Hannibal talked to General Camarillo for an hour or so while Amy and Face wandered back to their assigned rooms. They deliberately got lost several times looking around the presidential palace for the place where Nola Frame was being kept.

'There are only two places guarded in the residential part of this palace,' Amy told Hannibal when he joined them. 'One is Camarillo's personal quarters and the other one people just didn't want to talk about.'

'We'll go for it,' Hannibal said. He looked at his watch, then out at the approaching twilight. 'About now Murdock should be making a special night flight in the one aircraft B.A. will have left operational. Now we have to do our part.'

'Which is?' Amy asked.

'Profit by the confusion. But let's hurry. Camarillo wants us to come to dinner and we'll be trapped there.'

'This'll only work if Murdock gets the plane,' Face reminded him. 'And the plane is armed.'

'Don't tell me that you think someone *wouldn't* give Howling Mad Murdock a fully armed fighter plane?' Hannibal asked innocently.

'They might if he starts talking like Jimmy Cagney or Captain Midnight,' admitted Face.

'See? Nothing to worry about.'

Things get cracking on page 48.

From page 24.

The jungle was dimly lit. High overhead the trees interlocked, letting only spots of sunlight get to the ground, where rotting bits of vegetation, roots, and an occasional snake impeded their progress.

'Take it easy, B.A.,' Murdock protested. 'I'm a tenderfooted flyboy, remember?'

'Come on, fool. We ain't got all day. They'll miss those soldiers soon and go looking.'

'But I'm only human . . . .'

'Shut up,' B.A. growled. 'Move your feet, And don't get shot 'cause Hannibal is going to need you to fly outta here.'

'I'll try not to get shot,' Murdock said, tripping over a root. 'I may break a leg, though.'

One hour later, B.A. and Murdock crouched behind a bush, watching a sauntering native approach. Then the young man gasped as a big black man covered in chains of gold with the strangest hair he had ever seen loomed up before him. 'Where's this San Pietro prison?' B.A. asked him.

'Uh . . . uh . . . uh . . .'

B.A. grabbed him. 'The prison—where is it?'

The lad said something in Spanish, but B.A. just shook him. 'Speak American!'

'He doesn't *know* any, B.A.' Murdock blurted. To the youth he said, '¿*Donde está la prision de San Pietro?*' The boy chattered a moment and pointed. 'That stone building on the hill there,' Murdock said.

'Well, don't just stand there, let's go,' B.A. snapped.

The cells were small and dirty. There seemed to be a lot of them, and the only light came from a single string of bare light bulbs strung along the ceiling on nails driven into the old stones. Hannibal, Amy, and Face had separate cells but they could talk to each other.

'It's my fault,' Hannibal said. 'I should have got us a better cover.'

'You couldn't have known they'd have their ambassador check out IPC,' Face said.

'I *should* have thought of that,' Hannibal said grumpily. 'I'm going to have to turn in my diploma from Famous Planners School.'

'But how do we get out?' Face said. 'We don't know where the girl is, or Murdock, or B.A.'

'If they caught the rest of the team they'd probably toss them in here,' Amy said. 'And interrogate us all together.' She crossed her arms around her body and shivered. 'I didn't like that colonel thinking we were guerrillas. Guerrillas do not get much in the way of human rights around here.'

But Hannibal wasn't really listening. He was looking at the electrical wiring.

A guard gets a nasty surprise on page 49.

From page 25.

They heard the loudspeaker switch on and the sneering voice of a man: 'Ah, the great A-Team has come to our little coastal country, no doubt to honour us with a display of bravado.' He laughed. It was not a pleasant laugh.

'Good evening, General. I don't know what this is about, but we came here to discuss business,' Hannibal directed his voice toward the group of men in the seats.

'Hah! You are mercenaries! Hired assassins! I know of you. Three months ago you stole a collection of priceless coins from Hernando Alvarez!' boomed the voice.

'But he had stolen them from our client, Barbara Dun—'

'*Silencio!* Four months ago you took a man from jail in Iran!'

Hannibal grinned. 'Yes, that really did frost their turbans, but they had put him there for singing "America, the Beautiful" . . . a nice song but a stupid place to sing it, considering.'

'Then you admit to being the A-Team!'

'Yes . . . part of it.' Hannibal took a button of his bush jacket and lifted it to his lips. 'Baker Team, are you ready?' He held the button to his ear, smiled, and then spoke again. 'Hold at zero minus three. Wait for my voice command. If there is no order after thirty minutes, execute Plan Omega.' He dropped his coat button and smiled winningly. 'We, um, have associates, General. Unless we are released and allowed to escort Señorita Frame to her father, I'm afraid your palace, all your records, *and* your vault will be destroyed!'

Hannibal plays a dangerous bluff on page 52.

From page 25.

Assisted by a loudspeaker, which sent his voice booming over the concrete ring, a man introduced himself. 'Good evening, Mister Hannibal Smith. On behalf of my country, let me welcome you and the A-Team to Costa Verde.'

'Would you like an autograph?' Murdock said, but Hannibal shushed him.

'Good evening, General. You seem to have the advantage over us. Good evening, Señorita Frame. You'll be happy to know your father is well and in the United States,' Hannibal spoke to the group in the stands.

There was some fuss near the microphone and the sound of a slap echoed across the arena. 'Ahem. Pardon me, Colonel Smith, but there are some women who have learned some very bad habits in your country. Now, fellow officers and, of course, Señorita Frame, we begin the entertainment for the evening.'

At once there was a rumbling at one end of the stadium. Before they could realize what was happening they suddenly saw three of the biggest men they had ever seen. The men had knives—big knives—and all of them looked very mean.

Hannibal was all business as he muttered orders so that their opponents couldn't hear him. Amy protested, 'Hey, what'll I do?'

'I want you to eek and scream. Get hysterical and act like all those heroines in the movies in the forties and fifties. However you do it, get over by Nola Frame and be ready to snatch her out of there. You can't fight these guys but you *can* fight! Now get to it!'

Her scream was quite good, building from a whimper to a gasping yelp.

The knives are out and cutting on page 51.

From page 28.

'I know where Nola is,' Face said to Hannibal when he got back to his room. 'I followed her down a hallway and had a chance to talk to a maid. She is there against her will, but the general is losing patience. With her father out of the country the general has lost his blackmail hold on her. It's her will against his. But her family is prominent—all the other prominent families were decimated during the last two revolts. So she is a *kind* of royalty and he wants that legitimacy. It's marriage or death for her—nothing else. He's given her two days to decide.'

Hannibal said, 'Then we must move at once. Fast. We'll use Plan B.'

'What's that?' Amy asked.

'I don't know. I just always wanted to say that.'

Clink.

The grappling hook was padded, but it still made a little noise. They had four minutes to scale the wall, pull up the rope, and get out of sight before the patrol returned. Hannibal and Face went up quickly, leaving B.A. to watch from behind. Amy had gone with Murdock to the airport to secure the Lear jet.

Working from a mental image of the layout, Hannibal and Face, dressed in black, went across the tile roof, then lowered themselves to Nola Frame's window. They saw her inside, crying. A silver letter opener lay prominently on the table next to her. Hannibal pointed at the knife, then made a phony smile and pointed to Face's face. He nodded, grimaced, and silently slipped the catch on the window.

 Nola finds a handsome rescuer on page 50.

From page 29.

Amy walked past the guards. Then she tripped and fell, painfully sprawling across the floor. The guards came to her aid at once, lifting her up. She gasped, then moaned, holding her ankle and biting back the tears. Then she seemed to notice her ripped clothes and grew embarrassed.

'Please,' she protested, pulling away. But she limped on her hurt ankle and grasped the shoulder of the nearest guard. 'Please, uh, is there a woman around? Men embarrass me.' She managed to blush as she looked at the guard she was clutching. 'Especially handsome men,' she sighed.

The guard said something in Spanish, and they knocked on the door they were guarding and spoke to someone inside. Amy was helped through the doorway, and two large women took her in tow, helping her into a large room, elaborately furnished, where she was put on a chair. They clucked and murmured and took off her shoe and began rubbing her ankle.

Amy looked around at the quarters: a central room with a fountain and an open roof, like a small patio, surrounded by bedrooms. The architectural style was distinctly Moorish. The Moors had occupied Spain for centuries, bringing with them the Arabic architecture, which had been adapted by the Spanish, before spreading to the Latin peoples in Central and South America. Amy saw several beautiful young women peering from doors, and she recognized Nola Frame at once.

The rescuers get into real trouble on page 53.

From page 29.

Hannibal looked at his watch. Amy had managed to get into the women's quarters where Nola Frame was kept, which was run much like a harem. *Murdock should have refueled, and B.A. should have got to the fighters. We're inside the palace. That part was easy. Getting out is always the hard part.*

Colonel John 'Hannibal' Smith looked at Templeton Peck, who raised his eyebrows. Hannibal nodded, then he reached into a secret compartment in Amy's secretarial briefcase and punched a pre-set button. Then Face opened the door and Hannibal walked briskly out, followed by the handsome young man.

The surprised guards had to trot to catch up with them. 'Señor! Señor! Where are you going?'

Hannibal didn't look back. 'My evening walk, of course. Mister Peck, you are lagging behind!'

'Yes, sir, of course, sir.' To the guards Face said, 'Come along if you wish, but hurry. Mister Hannibal likes a good long walk before dinner.'

'*Si,*' the guard said, looking uncomfortable. Hannibal walked with assurance into the palace gardens, down a dark path, and into a darker thicket. There was the sound of blows, a gurgle, two thuds, and Hannibal came out of the thicket carrying an M-16 rifle. Face came out, took Hannibal's gun, and added it to the one he openly carried, as if they had found the guns and were turning them over to the proper authorities. Now they were committed.

 Hannibal and Face break into the general's private harem on page 54.

From pages 30 and 31.

With Hannibal back from his conference with the dictator, Face and Amy told him what they had found out about the palace. 'I think we know where some women are living,' Amy said. 'Face found a side exit with only one guard, and no one seems to have found the, um, contents of my briefcase.'

Hannibal nodded and then looked out the window at the approaching twilight. 'B.A. should be at work soon. Murdock's ready by now. We only have to get a diversion going.'

'What if Nola isn't where we think she is?' Amy asked.

Hannibal grinned. 'Then we ad-lib.'

Face groaned. 'I *hate* it when we improvize.'

B.A. looked at the twilight from the crate where he was sleeping and sat up carefully, so that his numerous gold chains did not clink. Then he slipped out of the shadows and into the nearest hangar. There was one mechanic working on a jet engine. He had parts of it on the floor, doing B.A.'s work for him.

B.A. walked up behind him. 'Hey, fool!'

'Huh—' *Thunk*. The man dropped to the concrete without another sound. B.A. pulled out a screwdriver and opened the access panel on the nearest jet.

Hannibal looks down a gun barrel on page 55.
From a polite dinner to an impolite break-in on page 56.   45

Hannibal looked at his watch surreptitiously. *Murdock should be suiting up to fly. B.A. is sabotaging the ships. Amy is vamping the guards. Face is getting the gear ready.* He smiled. 'I love it when a plan comes together,' he murmured.

'Señor?'

'Oh, sorry, General. I was just thinking . . . you, that is, Costa Verde and IPC make a good team. It might not be inconceivable for us to consider . . . at a later date, of course . . . more, um, cooperative ventures. It's no secret that we need to establish a gasohol plant somewhere along this coast. You have abundant sugar cane, and the Mexican oil fields are not far distant. We might well consider a merger of the two to be *extremely* . . .' He smiled knowingly and saw the greed in the general's eyes. 'And I mean extremely profitable for both sides. May I suggest a Costa Verde corporation wholly owned by you . . . with whomever you wish . . . which might buy up land we select and lease it to IPC for our plant facilities? You might also invest heavily in sugar cane futures.'

Hannibal heard himself set the lures and baits which were keeping the general and his highest officers bright-eyed and attentive. *Actually, it is a pretty good idea,* Hannibal thought. *We do need gasohol. Well, the essence of good lying is to include as much of the truth as possible.*

He looked at his watch. *We have to know where Nola is or nothing works.*

Target found! Turn to page 57.
46 *The general has his own secret plot on page 58.*

From page 34.

'The ship's ready,' B.A. said. 'Checked it myself.'

'Excellent, my good man,' Murdock said airily. He was suited up in a borrowed flight suit and helmet and grinned broadly at B.A.'s scowl. He tossed over his shoulder one end of the long white scarf he had produced from a pocket. *Those brave lads of World War I had the right idea—flamboyance, image, courage,* he thought. *Not to mention open-cockpit airplanes, which is the only way to fly.*

Murdock strode importantly to the selected fighter and got aboard with a flourish. He gave a spirited thumbs-up gesture to the watching group of officers and mechanics and took the plane out onto the runway. B.A. turned quietly back to his 'inspection.' His scowl and manner kept away any of the curious mechanics. The officers he let watch; he had early discovered they knew nothing at all about anything more mechanical than a doorknob.

B.A. looked at a clock on the wall. *Time's beginning to crowd in,* he thought. *I hope Crazy Murdock doesn't decide to sightsee.*

Three miles up, Murdock turned west toward the only other military airfield in the tiny country, the one at Santa Maria in a mountain valley. He was trying to remember how the cavalry bugled the charge, but all he could think of was John Wayne saying, 'Hu-oh!' He shrugged as the field became visible in the late-afternoon light.

'Hu-oh!' he said and started his dive.

Murdock attacks on page 68.

Hannibal stopped at the junction of the corridors. He took a quick look around the corner, then pulled back. 'It's just as you described it,' he whispered to Face and Amy. 'Two guards, no one else in sight. Come on.'

They marched around the corner as if late for an appointment. 'Ms Milton, tell Simpson at Base Metals that I want his report on pseudo-gravity restraints by Tuesday. Inform Warren at the Los Angeles plant to watch quality control on the Greenberg robotronics. Good evening, gentlemen,' he said to the guards, who had come to attention. 'I want Miller at L.A.S.F.S. informed of this merger with ITT PDQ. And . . . oh . . . ' He stopped and looked around. 'I think we've lost our way.'

Face turned at once to the guards. 'Señors, which is the way to the general's dining room?'

'No, no, no,' Hannibal said, walking up. 'We are dining in the State Dining Room, Androchak. That is right, isn't it, Ms Milton?' Hannibal turned toward Amy, then spun back, his fist slamming into the face of the guard. Face thumped the other guard just as quickly. They dragged the men into the suite as Amy shoved the big carved door open for them.

'What is the meaning of this?' a woman's voice demanded.

'Who are you?' Amy asked. The woman was tall, aristocratic, and beautiful.

'I am Nola Frame, and who are you? What has happened to my guards?'

'We are here to rescue you,' Face said.

And Nola Frame began to scream.

 The A-Team gets a surprise on page 59.

From pages 38 and 39.

While B.A. and Murdock were advancing through the jungle toward the prison, some soldiers had discovered the guards which B.A. had disposed of earlier. General Geraldo Camarillo was informed that the American imposters had been taken into custody. Nola Frame sat bleakly at her window in the presidential palace, meditating on her fate. And John 'Hannibal' Smith was making up an improvised hook from his and Face's shoelaces and a piece of metal torn from his bunk.

It took nineteen tosses, but at last he caught the metal over the electric line and began tugging the line loose from the ceiling. It was a difficult job to do with the shoelaces, but bit by bit he popped loose the nails from the crevices of the old slabs of stone. Finally he could reach out and grasp the electric wire and pull it in.

'It's in series,' he told the others. 'We can blow the lights anytime we want. But first, I've got to make a little trap.'

Hannibal carefully stripped the insulation from the old wiring, using a dime accidentally left in his pockets after the inspection. He explained his plan to Face and Amy, then unscrewed a light bulb. At once everything went black. He heard mutterings from the guards far down the corridor in the guard room. In a few moments one came down, lighting matches awkwardly as he held his automatic gun.

'Come on,' Amy said. 'Please, it's scary in here!'

The guard complained, but as he drew opposite Hannibal's cell the bare electric line was shoved toward him. The bulb was screwed in, lighting things up, and the guard screamed.

It's smash and grab on page 60.
B.A. gets ready to attack a fortress on page 61.   49

From page 42.

'Good evening, Señorita,' Face said in poor Spanish. Nola's head snapped up and she stared at the black-clad figure coming in her third-storey window. 'Don't be afraid. We're here to help you.'

He is handsome, she thought. *Just like a hero. Just like the books, coming in the window at the last moment.* She smiled.

'Good evening, señor. May I have your name?' Her heart was thumping. *What did the rescued girls say at a time like this?*

'Your father sent us.' Her face fell. *I had hoped it was because he loved me, seeing my face in a passing carriage, perhaps.* Then she remembered that she had never actually been *in* a carriage. 'We've come to take you to the United States.'

'Very well,' she said calmly. She indicated her robe and nightgown. 'I must change.'

'Hurry, please,' Face said. What she changed into rather surprised him. She looked like a pirate: tight black trousers, boots, wide belt, blood-red blouse, and a rolled bandana holding back her hair. He couldn't help whistling for she looked very good, indeed.

She climbed the rope like a pro, and soon they were timing the patrol on the other side of the palace. Hannibal went down first, rappeling off the stuccoed walls, then Nola and Face followed him.

B.A. rolled up in a truck with the lights off, and they got in. 'Hit it,' Hannibal ordered, and the truck lurched forward and crashed through a fence, fishtailed, straightened out, and roared toward the airport.

They shoot their way out on page 113.

From page 41.

Amy put the back of her hand to her mouth and shuddered. She lurched backwards and fell, crawled back, then got to her feet and retreated a step at a time.

Meanwhile B.A. moved out first. 'Don't be greedy, B.A., there's enough for all of us,' Hannibal said as he stepped toward the centre giant. Murdock and Face started moving out to the side, drawing away the third man.

'Come on, fool,' B.A. said. 'Come at me with that knife of yours and I'll—' His words were drowned out by a rather prolonged whimpering scream from Amy.

'Hi, there,' Hannibal said to the giant. 'You come here often?' The giant swung his knife at Hannibal, who jumped back. 'Your mother did not teach you manners,' he said disapprovingly.

'Murdock,' Face whispered, 'if you have some really *good* idea of how to work on Goliath here, I'd be glad to hear it.'

'Certainly.' Murdock stepped forward and stuck out his hand. 'This contest is under the auspices of the Marquis of Queensberry, my good man, and—*awk!*' The knife sliced open Murdock's brand-new uniform shirt. 'Now what did you do *that* for, you uncouth barbarian? That was my brand-new chief pilot's suit and—' He ducked as another knife thrust nearly got him. 'All right, if that is the way you greet tourists, very well! Prepare yourself for combat, sir!'

Amy screamed again as the biggest of the gladiators charged at B.A.

The knife fight continues on page 63.

From page 40.

The general's laugh over the loudspeaker was thunderous. 'You bluff, *Americano*! You have no compatriots. I would know!'

Hannibal smiled knowingly. 'Oh, is that right? Just as you know exactly which of your colonels is plotting against you? We know, because we were given that information by our contacts before we left the States! So if you don't know which colonel it is, how can you be *certain* there is no B-Team?'

There was a short silence, then a lot of chatter in the background.

'*Silencio*! We—'

'But General, he bluffs! How can there be—'

'—not one of us, I assure you, my general! The thought is unthinkable!'

'How did you know?' Amy asked.

'I didn't, but there are *always* ambitious colonels.' He raised his voice and called out to the group. 'General! There is little time. If my men move out of the range of my transmitter, I'm afraid I have no way to call them back!'

There was more confusion and noise. Hannibal boldly motioned the A-Team forward and they approached the stands. 'General,' he called out again. 'All we want is the young woman! Give her to us and we'll be gone.'

'But she—' The general looked at the dark-haired beauty as the A-Team moved closer to her.

Nola Frame stood up. 'General, I do not want to see anyone hurt, nor the palace destroyed. That is the heritage of the people of Costa Verde! I will go with these people in the name of peace!'

 Hannibal's bluff continues on page 62.

From page 43.

Amy looked at her watch. B.A. had sabotaged the fighters, Hannibal had got rid of the guards. Now she had to get out and tell them how to get back in without a fuss. But first . . .

She got up and, against the protests of the old women, hobbled toward the surrounding wall, as if trying out her ankle. She came up to the door where Nola Frame stood and seemed to collapse against the beautiful young woman. 'You are going to be rescued,' she whispered into the ear of the startled woman. 'We know your father. We'll be back in a few minutes—tell no one!'

'I think I'm better now,' Amy said and limped to the door. She smiled at the handsome guard, who smoothed his moustache and leered. Then she limped off down the hall.

Amy gave them the layout in Hannibal's room. 'Over or through?' Face asked.

'Over. Get the nylon ropes,' she answered.

Thin, strong ropes with folding hooks were taken from secret compartments in the suitcases. In a few minutes they had found their way onto the palace roof and to the open patio. Hannibal and Face silently slipped down and found Nola's room. She was waiting, trembling and wide-eyed.

Face smiled at her and bowed. 'Señorita,' he murmured, all his obvious appreciation in his eyes and smile. She went with him as though in a dream. Hannibal stood back and let Templeton Peck climb to the roof, then pull up the scared girl.

Then an old woman appeared, screamed, and the two guards burst into the room.

Shots fired! Car chase! Getaway! Turn to page 94.

From page 44.

Hannibal walked briskly up to the first guards he saw—which happened to be those guarding the women's quarters. He indicated Templeton Peck, lumbering along behind him, awkwardly trying to carry the two M-16s.

'You,' Hannibal said in his parade colonel's voice. The guards stood at attention. 'I found these in the garden! Is it the policy of your army to leave weapons just lying around? Mister Peck, give these enlisted men these weapons and get a receipt!'

'A receipt, señor?' asked the befuddled guard.

'Here,' Face said, bundling the guns into the man's hands.

'Oh, all right,' Hannibal grumbled. 'I'll give you something.' His fist thudded into the other guard's jaw only two seconds before Face's fist punched the first guard out. They couldn't catch all the bodies or weapons and there was a clatter.

Enough of a clatter, it turned out, for the old woman to unlock the door and look out. In seconds Hannibal and Face were inside, being called over by Amy, who had found Nola among the dozen or more beautiful young women the general kept there. Amy had got in by faking a twisted ankle right in front of the guards, but now she was perfectly healthy.

Face took Nola Frame's hand and kissed it. 'Señorita, if I had known of your beauty, we would have done this for nothing.' He ignored Hannibal's snort, and they rushed from the rooms, with their guns at the ready.

From page 45.

Hannibal, Amy, and Face had all changed into black clothes, sleek and tight-fitting, without loose parts to snag on things. Each had an equipment belt. Face and Hannibal had .45 automatics—flat guns which could easily be concealed in luggage; Amy had a tranquilizer gun.

'Time,' Hannibal said as he counted down the seconds on his watch. Face pressed a button on a small radio transmitter. At once they heard an explosion on the other side of the palace where Amy had 'accidentally' left her briefcase in the office of the Minister of Cultural Affairs. It was a pressure bomb—lots of smoke and noise but not much damage.

'Go.' They went out the tall windows and along the wide ledge, invisible in the night. They found the wing which they assumed was the women's quarters. And they found the iron grilles which covered all the windows.

'Thermit,' Hannibal said, and they set to work putting a thick string of the chemical compound around each of the four braces. Face strung the charges together and then backed along the wall before he ignited it. There were a few seconds of fiery light and sparks while the iron grille was eaten through by the intense heat. Then the grille fell into the bushes below.

In seconds Hannibal was through the unlocked window, gun in hand, to find six terrified young women staring at him. Six terrified women and one who wasn't: she had a gun pointed shakily at him.

The A-Team gets a nasty surprise on page 64.
They run for it on page 65.

There was a knock at the door of the guest suite. A smiling and handsome Captain Mendoza was there. He bowed to Amy, who almost blushed. 'The general requests the pleasure of your presence at dinner, gentlemen and . . . lady.'

'We'd be delighted,' Hannibal said.

'This throws our schedule off,' Face said when Mendoza had gone.

'Ad-lib,' Hannibal said and smiled.

The dining hall was huge. Banners, flags, portraits, and armour from the time of Cortez and Pizarro adorned the walls. Amy was the only woman there and very conscious that she was the focus of many eyes. Hannibal was seated on the right side of the dictator and Amy on his left. He often looked at her while he talked with Hannibal.

The talk between Camarillo and Hannibal was of money, business, and economic future, but when the general talked to Amy it was of her beauty, the beauty of Costa Verde, and the great food of the Central American country.

When they had returned to their rooms, Amy fumed. 'Why didn't he talk money to me and food to you? That . . . that . . . dictator!'

Hannibal looked at his watch. 'Well, shall we go see if our Señorita Frame is where we think she is?'

Twenty minutes later, dressed in black, they were on the ledge outside the patio window of the section cut off from the rest of the palace. 'There she is,' Amy whispered.

They find Nola, but . . . Turn to page 66.
56 *Nola turns everything around on page 67.*

From page 46.

Amy strolled along the high, wide corridors of the big presidential palace, inspecting paintings, looking out of windows into the patio, smiling at guards, dancing in circles before gilt mirrors, and generally acting just as flighty, foolish, and friendly as she could. Guards smiled and slicked down their manly moustaches. Passing officers offered their services as escorts. An enlisted steward offered her wine.

Amy told Face back in their suite what she had discovered. 'I narrowed it down to two places—both suites, both guarded. Then I saw a corporal taking in some freshly pressed uniforms, so that must be Camarillo's suite. The other, just down the hall, *should* be Nola's. It's a guess,' she shrugged, 'but what else do we have going for us?'

'Sometimes you just have to go with your feelings,' Face said, looking at his watch. 'Hannibal should be finished by now.'

A few moments later John 'Hannibal' Smith strode into the suite, puffing on a Monte Cristo cigar. His raised eyebrows were a signal for them to fill him in. 'We'll go with it,' he said, 'as soon as it is dark outside.'

'I hate waiting,' Face said.

'Think Murdock did his part?' Amy asked.

'He may be crazy,' Hannibal said, 'but he isn't stupid. He did his part.'

Murdock strikes on page 68.

From page 46.

General Camarillo looked at his officers. 'It sounds very good,' he offered.

Brigadier Ortega frowned. 'Too good?'

Major Montoya spoke up. 'Sir, these multinationals, they operate big. We are Costa Verde, true, but a company like IPC must own more property around the world than all of Costa Verde.'

Captain Ruiz looked puzzled. 'I don't recall exactly where I know this company. They all have initials . . . you have checked them out, sir?'

General Camarillo nodded. 'I cabled our ambassador at the United Nations. He is checking them out now. But there is no need to worry. If they do not appear to be what they seem, or if they attempt to change the deal, we nationalize them.' He smiled his alligator smile. 'Nationalization . . . such a nice term. Legal theft.' He laughed with his officers.

Camarillo's thoughts turned to the beautiful Nola Frame, the only one to resist him so far. *Perhaps,* he thought, *she only resists me because it intrigues me. It cannot be that she is not attracted to me.*

58   *Murdock, the one-madman air force, attacks on page 68.*

From page 48.

Hannibal stopped Nola's scream by grabbing her, but she struggled and almost got free. 'You don't understand,' Face said insistently. 'Your father hired us to bring you out, to take you to him. Now stop fighting me and—'

She broke her mouth free of his grip and snapped at him, 'Let go of me, you fool! You can't get me out! I don't *want* to get out!'

'You don't want to—' Face looked surprised.

'You know my father?'

'Yes!' insisted Hannibal.

'Then leave me. You don't understand what is happening here!' She looked around. 'I am with the guerrillas! I'm a plant! I will sabotage things here when our glorious freedom fighters attack!'

'When is that?' Hannibal asked.

'Tonight, you idiot! You'll spoil everything! Now go! I will keep the guards here some way. Get out before they find you!'

'Why tonight?' Amy asked.

'Because I thought you would distract the general,' she sneered, 'with his dreams of glory and money! Of power! Tonight we will take back our country!'

'Y'know, Face, sometimes I can't tell sides without a scorecard,' Hannibal sighed, releasing her. 'Revolt, counterrevolt, politics . . . ' He wiped his face. 'Okay, what can we do to help?'

'Help? You'll help us?' Nola asked.

Hannibal nodded. 'Before you say it, Face, you're right—I don't know what I'm doing,' Hannibal Smith said.

Nola sets a trap on page 69.

Murdock and B.A. blast a base on page 70.

From page 49.

The surge of power knocked the guard out. He fell toward Amy's cell. She grabbed him, tugged him closer, and groped for the keys. They could hear the other guards coming down the long hall, cursing in the darkness. Amy found some keys, but it took her precious moments to find the right one to open her door. She threw the keys across to Hannibal. He only had time to unlock his cell. He hid the keys in his pocket, then he ordered Face and Amy to stand back in their cells as if they were all still locked up.

'I don't know what happened,' Hannibal said to the two guards who stumbled in. 'He tried to fix the wiring but blew it out.' Face made similar protests, anything to keep the guards from looking into Amy's cell. One guard bent over their downed comrade and the other peered angrily in at Hannibal.

Then Amy swung open her cell door, smashing it into the kneeling guard's head. When the other turned, Hannibal kicked his door open, knocking down the guard. A few well-placed blows in the dark silenced them. Moments later they were free and in the guard room, helping themselves to weapons.

'Well, subtlety and ruse are now obsolete,' Hannibal said. 'Now it's smash and grab.'

The A-Team makes a break for it on page 71.

60   *B.A. and Murdock break into prison on page 72.*

From page 49.

B.A. looked gloomily at the prison. It was an old fortress, with all the traditional defences of old fortresses. A stone prison was not too much protection against modern weaponry, but to two men armed only with stolen World War II Garands a fortress was pretty formidable, especially in daylight.

B.A. checked the sun. 'Not too long until dark. Let's go get some rope and stuff.'

'You're going to attack *that*?' Murdock said.

B.A. grabbed the pilot's shirt front. 'Are you saying I'm crazy, crazy?'

'Uh, no, B.A., I just thought there might be some more, ah, subtle method.' He smiled weakly.

'Such as?'

'Oh . . . uh . . . let me go, will you? Oh, well, you know all those movies where the hero lets himself get caught so he can get inside and free his friends and stuff?'

'That's movie nonsense, man. Real guards aren't all that dumb.' He did look thoughtful, though. The A-Team had been in a maximum security United States Army stockade, with very alert, professional guards. They had still got out of there. However, this was a banana republic, with sloppy soldiers who had outdated equipment and who probably had not seen very many movies.

'Ah, you're thinking,' Murdock said and grinned. 'That craziness you got must be spreading, man.'

Murdock brings in B.A. under guard on page 73.

The general dithered. He wanted Nola to stay, and he didn't believe the A-Team's boast, but he couldn't make a decision. It was the kind of decision he had never made. All his life it had been simple: go for the power. But if the palace were destroyed the people would hate him. They hated him enough now, but the palace was the single architectural boast of all of Costa Verde, for no Aztec or Mayan had ever built there in centuries past. The palace was the embodiment of Costa Verde's history. Its destruction could be the deciding factor with the majority of people who were not on his side.

'Go!' he said. He could not let it be said that his personal desires caused national tragedy. He might even be able to turn it to his advantage—his great love he gave up for his country. 'Go!'

Hannibal spoke into his jacket button. 'Baker-Team, hold at zero minus three. Activate Plan E.' To the general he said, 'We'll take that armoured truck you have outside. We'll leave it in Lost and Found at the airport.'

'Go!' growled the general, who was having second thoughts.

The A-Team and Nola trotted up the steps, right past the angry guards with their machine guns, and piled into the armoured truck. 'What about their fighter planes?' Murdock asked.

'That's why we're driving in this,' Hannibal said.

Bullets whine on page 115.

From page 51.

This was not the first knife fight in which B.A. Baracus had ever been involved. He was quicker than the other man and dodged the knife, bringing his axelike hand down on the man's neck. He jumped over the unconscious gladiator to give a wild kick into the side of the man facing Hannibal, downing him.

'Hey, I was doing all right!' Hannibal protested.

'We've got no time for fun, Hannibal!' B.A. said as he took care of the final blow that put down the second gladiator. But as the fierce black man turned on the third, he saw there was no need. Murdock had thrown sand in his face, tripped the bellowing giant, then thumped him with the handle of his own knife.

In the meantime, Amy had climbed the steps, quietly cowering, and was not far from a soldier with a machine gun. She whimpered with fear, clung to his ears, then suddenly toppled the man. After grabbing the gun, she stood and sent a dozen rounds over the heads of the Costa Verde high command. 'Freeze! One shot and all these generals and colonels will be dog meat!' she yelled. At once the officers cautioned the guards not to fire. They cowered under the gun of the transformed Amy Amanda Allen.

'Good work,' Hannibal said as he ran up and took Nola's hand. 'We're borrowing your armoured truck, General! Thank you for an entertaining evening, but I wouldn't be putting those guys in the Olympics!'

The A-Team ran for the exit.

Turn to page 115.

From page 55.

'Easy,' Hannibal said. 'You're Nola Frame, aren't you?'

The woman hesitated. 'Yes? I don't know you.'

'Your father sent us to rescue you.' Face and Amy entered slowly through the window.

The young woman looked puzzled. 'But my father is dead.'

'No, he's alive,' Hannibal said. 'He paid us to take you away from here.'

'That can't be,' she insisted, still holding the small pearl-handled automatic on them. 'My father died a year ago. I was at the funeral. I saw him in his coffin.'

'Uh-oh,' Face said.

'Well, whomever he was, he paid us good dollars to take you out. Do you want to go?'

'Yes!' she said at once. She lowered the automatic. 'I smuggled this in. I was going to kill the general if he tried to . . . if he . . . '

'Yes, we understand,' Amy said. She looked at the other women. 'What about them, Hannibal?'

'Good question. Do any of you ladies want to get out of here?' They all did. Face groaned. Hannibal said, 'It's out the front, then.' They gathered the women together near the door, then Nola pushed it open.

'What kind of guards are you?' she yelled at them, coached by Hannibal. 'Look who you let get in here!' She pointed into the quarters and as the two guards came in, guns ready but their attention elsewhere, Hannibal and Face hit them.

 Hannibal tricks one of his best men on page 79.

From page 55.

'Oops! Easy there, señorita,' Hannibal said as Amy and Templeton Peck got in off the ledge, carefully watching the armed woman. 'I'm Hannibal Smith; this is Amy and the Face man. We've come to rescue Nola Frame.'

'I'm Nola Frame,' one of the women said in surprise. 'Did my father send you?'

Hannibal nodded and put out his hand for the gun. 'Uh, señorita, we can take all of you out if you want. To the United States? Away from here?' The woman looked scared and still covered them with the small automatic. 'We know you're scared, but I assure you that we are good, honest rescuers with no other motive. We're professionals.'

'She has the gun to kill the general,' Nola said. 'And then to kill us to save us from the fate his soldiers would inflict.' To the woman she said in Spanish, 'It is all right, Maria—these are friends.'

The woman slowly lowered the gun and everyone sighed. Hannibal indicated she should keep it, and he and Face went to the entrance to the wing and got ready. They swung the door open suddenly and snatched the guards in, muffling their yells, and Amy slammed the door closed. Hannibal and Face quickly changed clothes, and moments later they were herding the women, including Amy, out under the threat of their guns.

'We're taking them to safety,' Face said to a passing platoon sergeant. Getting out of the palace was no problem. They stole a truck and headed for the airport.

Murdock solves a problem on page 97.

From pages 27, 33 and 56.

With B.A. and Murdock off taking care of the Costa Verde Air Force, Amy, Face, and Hannibal had climbed along the palace wall, using the ledges in the dark, to locate Nola Frame's site.

Face slipped his knife blade under the catch on the tall French windows, and they crept over the sill. Nola Frame sat reading in a chair in a large room. What looked like several bedrooms opened off the central room. There was an old crone making lace in the corner under another light. A pair of pretty young women were idly playing cards at a table. None of them had noticed the three intruders.

Hannibal directed Face at the door to the wing, then gestured for Amy to go to Nola. He crept behind a sofa and toward the old crone. She, as *dueña*, or guardian, would be the one to get noisy.

But it was Nola who saw them first. Her eyes darted to Amy as the young American came toward her on all fours. Nola's eyes grew big with fear, but Amy put her finger to her lips and the girl hesitated. Amy crept to Nola's feet and motioned for her to bend over. 'I know your father,' she whispered. 'We're here to rescue you.'

'We?'

At that moment the old crone let out a screech.

From page 56.

Hannibal gently shoved the window open and all three of them slipped in quietly. Hannibal nodded approvingly at Amy's smooth moves. *She's beginning to shape up very well*, Hannibal thought as they reconnoitered the room. Nola seemed alone at first, but then they saw an old woman puttering about with leftover dinner dishes.

They impatiently waited until the crone had left, then Hannibal spoke softly from the shadows. 'Señorita . . .'

Nola Frame's head snapped up and she searched the room in quick looks. 'Who's there?' she demanded.

'Friends. Your father sent us to bring you to him.'

'My father?' She half rose from her seat, then sank back as Hannibal stepped from the shadows.

'Yes. We're the A-Team. He hired us to get you out of the clutches of General Camarillo.'

She looked bewildered. 'But . . . but *why*? I am going to marry him. I love him.'

Hannibal blinked and looked around at Face and Amy as they moved out from the shadows. Face said, 'You *love* him?'

'Yes, is that a crime? He is handsome and brave and the *president*.'

'You don't have to marry him because of that,' Amy said. 'The president part, I mean.'

'What is this?' The voice was that of General Camarillo, who stood in the open door. He drew his gun, as did the guards behind him. 'I think you are an imposter, señor.'

The dungeon is dark and cold on page 75.
They wait for the torturers on page 76.

From pages 47, 57 and 58.

Murdock zoomed in low, under the radar detection of the military base on the western edge of Costa Verde. His first bomb blew a large hole in the centre of the first runway. On his second pass he took out the other runway. After making the field impassable for the jets to get off the ground, he turned back toward San Felipe.

'Good job, Murdock,' he said pompously, 'Couldn't have done better myself.' He changed voices: 'Indeed, it was done in the best standards of the service.' His voice went high: 'I annoint thee Sir Murdock, Knight of the Realm.' His voice dropped and he assumed a Brooklyn accent: 'Hey, man, that was somethin' else!' In a nasal British accent he said, 'Good show, old boy!'

And no one hurt, he thought.

The headquarters at San Felipe went crazy. 'Guerrilla attack! Probably from a hidden airfield! Or out of those suspected secret bases in Costa Rica or Honduras! Go on red alert! We are under attack! Inform the general at once!'

Murdock turned on his microphone. 'San Felipe Control, this is Charles Lang. What's going on? I saw some kind of bombing back in the hills! Is there a war on? Don't shoot me when I come in to land, okay? Over.'

68 *Hannibal bluffs a dangerous man on page 104.*

Nola Frame took a map from a secret compartment in an ancient carved desk. She spread it out and pointed to several entrances to the palace. 'My compatriots will strike at the army base, at the docks, and the airfield.'

'Tell them not to bother with the airfield,' Hannibal said. 'We have already put it out of action.'

'But we do have one man—our man—up in a fighter,' Face said. 'Or he should be.'

'*Bueno*, I shall make a phone call,' Nola said.

'You can telephone a guerrilla force?' Amy asked.

'Communications are the heart of any army,' Nola said with conviction. 'Besides, they are in San Felipe. They have been filtering in for three days. The switchboard will listen in, of course, but I shall get the message across.'

The A-Team listened with delight as Nola called a 'brother' and chatted casually. When she hung up she smiled. '*Bueno*, they will have more people for the palace. Now, here's how you can help us.'

Hannibal strikes on page 78.

From page 59.

The lights of San Felipe were a complex dot pattern far below him. Although the landing lights were not on at the airport he could make out the hangars easily. Murdock looked at his watch. 'Let's hope they are all in their places with bright, shiny faces . . . Tallyho!'

The jet tilted over and began a bomb run straight at the main runway. He only had two bombs and there were two runways, so B.A. and Murdock had figured out how to do it.

The first bomb hit, triggering confusion, screams, alarms, and a great deal of running around. B.A. grinned fiercely as he yanked a gasoline truck driver out of his cab. He jumped in and drove it onto the unbombed strip, skidded it crossways, and jumped out. He hit running before Murdock's strafing run, which exploded the gas truck, got him.

'Crazy fool!' B.A. glared into the night. Then he started running toward the civilian field. There was one unbombed strip there. Sooner or later the people in charge would think of it and tear down some fences to get their fighters—*if* they could repair them in time—over there.

70   *A dangerous change of plans occurs on page 77.*

By careful stalking they got almost to the open air before they were discovered. An unarmed clerk carrying papers cowed under Hannibal's gun, and he showed them a direct way out of the prison. Soon they were on the outer wall, crouched in the shadows, the clerk tied up in an empty room below.

They had no rope, no way down. They didn't know where Nola Frame or Murdock and B.A. were, and General Camarillo knew they were phonies. 'We have nothing to lose,' Hannibal said and grinned.

'You know,' Face said, 'I wish you wouldn't make that kind of speech to the troops.'

'We'll use the flagpole rope,' Hannibal said. 'But we must take care of the guards, at least on this side.'

Face sighed. 'Someday, Hannibal, someday we are going to find a guard as good as we are.'

'Don't worry about it. If you were a guard on a pile of stone like this, would *you* be 100 per cent alert?'

'Small consolation,' Face muttered as he set out to eliminate his half of the guard force. Hannibal motioned Amy to stay as he set out for the other half.

There were a few rustling noises, a faint thud, and tinkle, but nothing in the twilight to disturb anyone. Then the Costa Verde flag fluttered to the stone deck and Hannibal was making a getaway rope from it.

He looped it over a weathered crenellation and dropped it into the darkness at the base of the wall. Face went over first, establishing a base, then Amy, and finally Hannibal.

Sneak attack on page 80.

From page 60.

They surprised the guards at the main gate, lounging in a guard room, and herded them below into cells, where Amy guarded them with a machine gun until Face and Hannibal took care of the guards at the exit. They whispered to her in a few minutes, and they all slipped out quickly.

The guards in the cells started yelling at once, but it took some time before anyone heard them and then reacted to the noise. After all, they were used to yells coming from the cells.

'What about B.A. and Murdock?' Amy asked as they trotted along the road into town.

'In time they'll go back to the jet and wait,' Hannibal said. 'But there's no predicting what either of them will do.'

At that moment B.A. and Murdock were cautiously approaching the main gate, intrigued by it's being left partially open. When B.A. saw the unconscious guards lying in the shadows, he grinned. 'Come on, fool, they ain't here.'

'But—'

'They've gone after the target.'

'Hey, wait for me!'

 The A-Team wears a disguise on page 80.

B.A. had his hands behind him, carefully holding the ends of the rope looped around his hands. He looked dejected and defeated as he limped along up the stone road to the main entrance of the fortress. Behind him, strutting like a peacock, holding an M-1 on the black man, with another rifle slung over his shoulder, was Howling Mad Murdock.

'Open up in there, poltroons. I have captured this varlet in classic combat, defeated his mighty thews and am bringing him to justice!'

'Don't overdo it, fool,' B.A. whispered fiercely.

The gate cracked open a few inches and a soldier looked out into the circles of light cast by the bulbs flanking the entrance. He ducked back, and a few moments later, as B.A. and Murdock arrived, a man with a peaked cap looked out.

'Ho there!' Murdock said loudly. 'I have a prisoner for you! Incarcerate him at once and inform the general!'

'Señor, who *are* you? You are an American, no?'

'Wrong! I am an American *yes!*' Murdock said with great bravado. 'I am General Geraldo Camarillo's *personal* anti-guerrilla advisor, specially flown in from the urban jungles of Pueblo de Nuestra Senora Reina de Los Angeles, better known as L.A. It is my expertise which has brought the perpetrator to the bar of justice! Admit us and give me a receipt for this one!'

The officer hesitated, then pushed the gate open.

That was his first mistake.

His second was to try and stop B.A. Baracus from eliminating him as a threat.

B.A. crashes on page 81.

From page 66.

Things happened fast then. Hannibal jumped up and put his hand over the old woman's mouth. The two young women playing cards dived under the table. Nola stood up; Amy pulled her down. Two guards crashed through the door, guns at the ready. Face tripped one, punched the other in the side of the head, then kicked the other with a karate move.

'Come on!' Hannibal said, releasing the old woman, who started squawking again. He leaped across the room, grabbing up Nola, who yelped, and they all ran out into the corridor. They turned left and raced for the exit to the parking lot.

There was a lot of yelling and commotion behind them. An alarm started to ring. 'Now!' commanded Hannibal, and Amy dug out her small radio transmitter and triggered it. On the other side of the palace, wedged halfway down the laundry chute to the cellar, the bomb in the briefcase went off, sending smoke, soot, dust, and noise up in a fountain. People started running the other way.

It took Face about fifteen seconds to hot-wire a jeep before they were off and running. Hannibal stood up and shouted orders to passing troops. Every order was contradictory, but he had that parade-ground voice, that air of command, and most of them obeyed him.

The airport and the next problem loomed up shortly afterward.

74   *The A-Team is under fire on page 98.*

From page 67.

The dungeon was damp and oddly cold, considering the climate. They put Amy in one cell and Face and Hannibal in another across the stone passage.

'Do you feel like this is *The Count of Monte Cristo*?' Face asked.

Amy put her arms over her head in a parody of all those dungeon cartoons and said, 'Now here's my plan.'

'Yes,' Hannibal said, 'we have them where we want them.'

There was a collective sigh, then Hannibal said, 'All right, let's see what we have. Empty your pockets and look the place over.'

Ten minutes later they realized they had a problem. The guards had taken their wallets, money, belts, shoelaces, and all weapons, including a knife strapped to Face's leg.

'Well, all right,' Hannibal said, 'let's see what our psychological tools are. B.A. and Murdock *may* be free, but the soldiers may have at least gone to collect them. They won't be easy to collect, of course, but Murdock will be hard to separate from the plane. If they don't arrive here in an hour or so, I think we can figure they are still loose.'

'Why did her father want to get her back?' Amy asked. 'Did he *know* she loved the general? If she does. And she appears to.' She sighed. 'The course of true love—or rescue—never runs true.'

Then they heard the rattle of chains and the clank of a steel door.

Worse trouble occurs on page 82.
Murdock arrives on page 83.

From page 67.

Hannibal, Face, and Amy were marched off to the dungeon, a very old and quite formidable prison. They were ordered to take everything from their pockets. As Hannibal pulled out his cigar lighter, he thumb-twisted the colonel's eagle fastened to the side.

Back at the Lear jet, Murdock heard a beeping from Hannibal's kit bag. He didn't waste time. He fired up the jet and was off and flying in minimum time. Then he started vectoring, using the faint signal from the sending device in the lighter to get a fix on where the colonel—or at least his lighter—was.

The guards put Face and Hannibal in one cell and Amy in another. General Camarillo frowned at them. 'Señor Hannibal, I do not know who you are, only who you pretend to be. But I think soon you will tell me. I have some very good questioners here.'

'If we say the secret word, do we get a prize?' Hannibal asked.

The general smiled thinly and smoothed his moustache in a thoughtful way. 'Yes. Your life. At least for a short time more.' The general looked at Amy, who glared with defiance. He bowed slightly and made his exit.

The two guards who watched them just grinned. 'The *Cachiporro* will be here soon. They were out in a village, talking to people.' They seemed to think that was very funny, and slapped each other on the back.

From page 70.

Murdock dropped the jet into a tight turn and headed down to land on the civilian side. He skidded the plane to the side of the strip and popped the canopy. Jumping out, he ran toward the Lear jet. Midway he passed the hard-running B.A., going for the jet.

'Good evening, sir!' Murdock called out. 'Nice night for a stroll, isn't it?'

'Fool,' growled B.A. He ran to the fighter and opened the fuel valves. High-test gasoline poured out, making a pool below the craft. B.A. snatched up a rock from the shoulder, wrapped a rag around it, and soaked it all in gas, choking on the fumes. Then he ran twenty yards, lit the gas rag, and threw the flaming mess toward the jet.

Whoomp!

The plane went up in a fireball. Ammunition exploded. B.A. ran for the Lear jet. *Get Hannibal and the others aboard and then head for the hills and walk out of here!* he thought.

The Lear coughed and the jet started warming up.

B.A. looked at the road but didn't see Hannibal.

The guerrillas hit on page 86.

From page 69.

Hannibal thought perhaps he was looking at his watch too much. It's not good for a leader to appear nervous or uncertain. Then he smiled. Right now he was a kind of deputy boss, because it was Nola Frame who was calling the shots in the palace.

Hannibal took one more peek around the corner. Two guards were at the door to the rear parking lot. Face was over by a side entrance, and Nola and Amy were going to take care of a single guard at the alarm centre. Each had his job. In less than a minute a number of guerrillas were going to pop out of the bushes and run like blazes toward the doors which he and Face had to liberate.

Hannibal took a deep breath and started around the corner, waving a bottle of the local liquid poison. He was singing 'The Yellow Rose of Texas' with enthusiasm if not skill. He offered either guard a drink. Both refused. But you know how drunks are, they get insistent. He good-naturedly collared one laughing and singing, and got a headlock and drove him into the stomach of the other.

He opened the heavy door about twelve seconds before the first guerrilla got to it. He charged right through with forty more behind him. No alarms went off. But there was certainly a big fight.

Hannibal didn't stay around to see who won. He collected Face and Amy and a protesting Nola and they went to the airport in a large hurry. The Lear jet was ready. Everything was ready except B.A. Baracus. 'I ain't going. You can't make me go,' B.A. grumbled. 'Now get out o' here, Hannibal!'

78   *B.A. is suspicious on page 106.*

From page 64.

Down the corridor they scampered, while across the palace firemen were pulling hoses through the halls. Face took care of the single guard, and in a few moments more they were in a government truck, Hannibal at the wheel, tearing through the evening streets toward the airport.

'Not her father, huh?' Face muttered to Hannibal.

'We'll figure that one out later. Now we have to figure out how to get B.A. on the jet.'

'Oh, good luck,' Face said.

They skidded to a stop. While Face and Amy tried to figure out how to get seven women and the A-Team into the small executive jet, Hannibal spoke to B.A., who assured him the fighter planes, at least the ones at this airport, were not going to be flying for some time.

'Now I'll be gettin' on,' B.A. said, eyeing the jet. 'Take the train back to the U S of A.'

'Without a passport, money . . . and the wanted posters?' Hannibal said. 'Half of Central America to walk through? Come on. B.A., come fly with us.'

'No way, man, I'm not flying, not with crazy Murdock.'

'Well, I guess this is the finish then, B.A. We'll probably not see you again.'

'Guess so.'

'Have a last drink, B.A. Toast the devil and lady luck,' Hannibal said. B.A. reluctantly agreed, and Hannibal fished a bottle out of his bag in the plane. It took five precious minutes for the drugged booze to work before they could pile the unconscious B.A. aboard.

The plot flips on page 109.

The presidential palace was a huge, sprawling building of Spanish-Moorish design, built in the mid-1800s when Costa Verde had been part of a neighbouring country. It seemed well guarded with soldiers but, as Face pointed out, the guards at service entrances were less alert, because of the constant comings and goings of cooks, bakers, delivery men, maids, and so on.

Hannibal and Face stole some white butcher's clothes from a van and put them on. Then they hefted slabs of fly-specked meat to their shoulders and walked right past the sleepy and indifferent guards.

'If I was post commander, I'd have their hides,' Hannibal muttered. 'Let's find a maid.'

'Why a maid?' Amy asked. 'Because she would likely know where Nola was kept?'

The frightened young woman they pulled into a linen closet spilled everything at once, speaking a mixture of Spanish, Indian, and pidgin English. Third-floor room in northwest corner.

They tied her up and gagged her as gently as they could, then dumped their butcher's clothes for the black-and-white livery of the servants. Using a stack of towels to hide their faces, they went boldly to the third floor.

Nola Frame's room was guarded by sleepy soldiers, who went right into more sleep, courtesy of two hard fists. Dumping the laundry, Hannibal led the A-Team into the suite. The first person he saw was an officer with a dapper moustache and a surprised look. Hannibal pointed his stolen .45 at him. 'General Camarillo, I presume?'

The general suffers more than just an indignity on page
80   *110.*

From page 73.

'Colonel!' B.A. said as he charged into the darkened corridor.

'Here, B.A.!'

'What's going on here, Hannibal?' B.A. grumbled as he felt his way into the darkened hall, the keys in his hand.

'I, uh, made a miscalculation. The wire knocked the guard out all right, but he didn't have the keys on him and the other guards took him away and said they'd be back to beat us up.'

'No, they won't,' B.A. said, sticking a key into the cell lock. 'We gotta move fast. We only got these guards and the ones at the gate. There are guns in the guard room.'

'Thanks, B.A.,' Amy said and gave him a hug. In the dark he permitted himself a look of surprise, but he did feel pretty good as he led them out into the free air.

Nola's father, Manuel Frame, had been certain that Nola was being held in the presidential palace, so it was there that they rushed. Hannibal outlined a plan and asked B.A. if he thought he could do it. B.A. just looked at him like he was a fool. They all got out of the stolen truck and crept into the gardens.

B.A. gave them time enough to get around to the side, then started up the truck and drove it sedately up the curving drive to the front. At the last minute he gunned it, shoved a rock against the accelerator, and dived out as the big army truck bounced up the steps and smashed into the entrance. It was bullet-riddled by the terrified guards, but it had done its job of distraction.

A knockout is staged on page 111.

From page 75.

Into the dungeon came General Camarillo and Nola Frame. They stopped before the cells and everyone looked at everyone else. 'Sorry we can't offer you a glass of wine,' Hannibal apologized, smiling.

'Señor, you betrayed the trust of Costa Verde,' the general said.

'You were willing enough to line your pockets,' Hannibal said, pointing his finger.

'I had you checked out before you landed and knew that there was no IPC, that you were false, so I decided to play along and see what you were up to.' He put his arm around Nola. 'You attempted to steal my heart!'

'Our mistake,' Face said. 'Her *father* thought you had abducted her.'

'Impossible!' the general said, frowning fiercely. 'It was for her protection!' Nola nodded agreement. 'There are those who would get at me through her.'

'Communists!' Nola said sharply.

'Well, you got into power the way of the midnight coup,' Face pointed out.

'Did you know the regime before us?' the general demanded. 'Butchers! Fascists! Evil men! I am about to declare that an election will be held in six months.' 'Okay,' Hannibal said, 'we made a mistake. But you can understand a father's concern. . . .'

'Of course. That will be taken into consideration during your trial.'

 B.A. makes a vital decision on page 87.

From page 75.

It was a platoon of nervous soldiers with Murdock in the middle. He was singing 'La Marseillaise' in a stirring way, then jabbered like a monkey as they put him into the cell next to Amy. Murdock climbed the bars, chittered and spat, scratched himself, then dropped to the floor.

'You may go, men,' he said in a British accent. 'Jolly good of you to see me home.' He gave them a stiff British salute and held it rigidly until they backed away and left. Then he brought down his hand, dug into his jacket pocket, and took out a key. He bent over, hunched his shoulder, and said, 'Master! Master! I have the key, Master!'

'Is it the *right* key?' Hannibal asked.

Igor was gone and he was an unabashed kid again. 'Gee, Colonel, I dunno, gosh.'

'Well, *try* it!' Face hissed.

'Gee, what do you know, it works,' Murdock said, swinging open the cell door. 'I wonder if it locks, too?' He closed the door and locked himself in again.

'*Murdock!*' Face yelled.

'Oh, okay.' In a few moments they were free. 'B.A. loused up their planes good. He wasn't back, though, when they came for me.'

'I want to have another talk with Señorita Nola,' Hannibal said. They all made their way through the darkened palace, hiding from a trio of passing soldiers, and then disposed of the guards at Nola's door.

Love strikes from an unexpected angle on page 88.

From page 76.

Murdock cruised at 8,000 feet, checking his gasoline supply. No fighters had come up after him, so he assumed B.A. had done his job. He had command of the air, at least for the moment, but in an unarmed plane.

Murdock dived down toward the palace, then angled off and flew low over the civilian and the military sections of the airport. People were shooting at him with handguns and a few rifles, but he knew how hard it was to hit a flying object in the dark. It took him two passes before he saw B.A., standing in a patch of light.

Murdock did a third pass, waggling his wings to indicate acknowledgement, and went straight for the palace. He assumed that B.A. would do something, would know something had gone wrong.

Now it's up to me to keep these fellas busy, Murdock thought. He grinned and heeled over, roaring past the control tower only a few feet away. He saw the controllers dive for the stairs, and he lanced up into the evening sky and began searching for targets of opportunity.

Fool! B.A. thought to himself as he ran in a steady pace toward the palace. *He likes flying like that, no rules, taking chances. It was guys like that that gave me this complex about flying.* B.A. squinted up into the sky. *I don't care if he was a Blue Angel precision pilot at one time—they threw him out because he scared them, too.*

He ran on, a big mean man with friends in trouble.

B.A. does the unexpected on page 89.
B.A. attacks on page 90.

Thwack! Hannibal struck first.

Thud! Face took out his guard almost as quickly.

The guerrillas arrived at the opened door only seconds later. They ran through, took up defensive positions, and motioned more from the bushes. The leader looked curiously at the two Americans. 'Who are they?' he asked Nola.

'Friends. They have arranged for a fighter to strafe the army barracks and keep people bottled up,' she said.

'Hah. Only for a few moments,' he sneered.

'Moments are sometimes all you get,' Hannibal said and smiled. 'Nola, won't you introduce us?'

'This is Ricardo Martinez, but I don't know your—'

Hannibal introduced everyone. They heard a jet scream low over the palace, then the stuttering of guns. 'Pass the word—the plane is ours,' Martinez shouted. 'Come, Nola, it is your right to be in at the finish!'

General Camarillo made his last stand in the president's office, but when two machine gunners burst through the door, he dropped his pistol and cowered. 'I'll pay you! I'll make you rich! Let me make you very, very rich!'

'With whose money?' Ricardo asked, a gun in his hand.

B.A. tries a trick on page 108.

Hannibal quickly outlined what Murdock and B.A. were doing or about to do. 'I have a radio here,' Nola said. 'I can contact him. We can use a fighter plane!'

She opened a closet and shoved aside some clothes. She opened a small compartment in the back and switched on a radio. Consulting a small sheet of paper, she dialed the combat frequency and Hannibal took the microphone. 'Murdock! Come in, Murdock. This is Hannibal, do you read me?'

'Hello, hello, I hear voices in my ears! Better than voices in my head, hey, Colonel?' Murdock's voice answered.

'Murdock, listen—you recognize my voice?'

'Betcha, Colonel, but maybe you better just give me some info to verify, something only maybe you and I know. Over.'

'That bar in Saigon, the one with the dancers. Who got you out of the dressing rooms and smoothed over the MPs?'

'You, my liege! Little *moi* had his trousers caught in a wringer that night!'

'All right, here's the change of plans. I want you to strafe the guard posts along Calle Guiterrez and keep the soldiers at the base from bothering us.'

'*Oui, mon colonel!* Jolly good show! Anything else, sir?'

'No, at least I don't think so. Try not to hurt anyone, just keep their heads down.'

'Roger. This is Captain Freedom making his glorious battle. I'd like my statue to be in pigeon-proof bronze, Colonel.'

86   *The guerrilla chief acts on page 85.*

From page 82.

After the general and Nola had departed, there was a long silence. 'Thought of anything?' Face asked from the bunk.

'That fleas are not good neighbours,' Hannibal responded.

'Well, I think we should . . .' Amy stopped as they heard a click. Then a scrape. Then the padding of stocking feet and the appearance of B.A. Baracus. The key ring jingled in his hand.

'Come on, let's get out o' this country,' B.A. said.

'I'm with *you*!' Face said.

They were quiet going up the steps. The palace was asleep. The two guards lay in untidy heaps in the shadows. They started for the nearest exit but Hannibal stopped them. 'I want one more little chat with Señorita Frame.'

'Aw, come *on*, Hannibal,' B.A. grumbled. 'That crazy Murdock is leading the Costa Verde Air Force in a crazy chase over the back country, up and down ravines and things. He'll be back any moment. We don't wanna miss him!'

'Go get us a car or something,' Hannibal said. Face sighed and motioned for Amy to go with Hannibal while he went with B.A.

Nola's eyes opened large again as she awoke with Hannibal's hand over her mouth. 'I'd like another talk,' he said and smiled.

Murdock's in a dogfight on page 91.

From page 83.

Nola was still shaking from being awakened by a hand across her mouth. 'No, señors, I assure you that I am *not* being held here against my will. I truly love the general and I shall make him a good wife. Costa Verde has not had a man like him in charge for decades. He *will* declare elections. I know it in my heart. He has promised me.'

'Women in love have been blind before,' Hannibal said.

'Yes, I know, and I know what some think. But they are the communists, who never like anything. They are the ones who profited from the old regimes. They would be glad to see my future husband brought down.'

'I hate to go home empty-handed,' Hannibal said. 'Amy, get some paper.' He handed Nola the paper and pen and said, 'Write your father and tell him.'

'We better skedaddle soon,' Murdock whispered, and Hannibal nodded.

'Here, señor,' Nola said. 'Take my ring as well. He gave it to me on my fourteenth birthday. He will know the letter is from me. I will stay here. Tell him he is wrong about Geraldo.'

'Now to find B.A.,' muttered Hannibal as they left the palace, slipping through the shadows.

'And get him on the plane,' added Face.

88 *B.A. makes a sudden appearance on page 92.*

From page 84.

Hannibal's head came up from the bunk as he heard the scuffle at the door. Then it was thrown open by the flying bodies of two screaming soldiers. The two guards stood up, disoriented, coming out of their half-sleep, but they were not fast enough for B.A. Baracus.

The hefty ex-sergeant charged through, punched one out and then took the rifle away from the other one and clubbed him down. Grumbling, he searched around, found the keys, and came across the stone floor in his combat boots and unlocked Hannibal's cell.

'What're you doing in here, Hannibal? You ain't supposed to get caught like this. I better think over our arrangement. I don't want to rescue fools any more than I got to.'

'Good job, B.A.,' Hannibal said and grinned. They released Amy and were running up the stairs to ground level in less than a minute. 'I caught me one of them guards and he told me you were down there,' B.A. said. 'Now let's get out o' here, Colonel.'

'Sergeant Baracus, we still have a mission to complete.'

'Ah, Hannibal,' moaned Face. 'They're on to us. They caught us and we are definitely lucky to be alive.'

'We took a mission, Face. Now let's go see this princess in the tower.'

'You're as crazy as Murdock,' B.A. muttered.

Amy's artistic performance begins on page 93.

From page 84.

B.A. looked through the bushes at the presidential palace. He had found people had a tendency not to guard rear and service entrances as well as the front ones. Perhaps because there would be too much interference with cooks, maids, delivery men, and so on. He moved closer.

Even at this hour of the evening there was some activity. A delivery van pulled up, and the driver took something inside. B.A. darted to the van and took a box and heaved it to his shoulder. This was the kind of time he wished that he did not make such a distinctive physical statement. He got some looks but no one, not even the idling, smoking guards, tried to stop him.

Inside he found a closet and waited until a single guard walked by. The man suddenly found himself in a closet, being held in the steel grip of a huge, bizarrely dressed man with the most ferocious scowl he had ever seen. It didn't even occur to him to mislead the man with the funny haircut. Getting punched unconscious was almost a blessing.

People generally do not try to get *into* prisons, and the guard at the top of the stairs to the dungeon was not too awake. B.A. threw him through the dungeon door and followed through in his usual bull-in-the-china-shop manner.

He grumbled at Hannibal as he released him from the cell and then shook his head as Hannibal announced they were going back after Nola Frame.

 Amy goes out of character on page 93.

From page 87.

'I had to say that,' Nola said. 'He knew you were not who you seemed to be. This place has insects.'

'Bugs,' Amy said. 'Electronic bugs. Listening devices.'

Nola nodded. 'I have been delaying him, stalling for time.' She smiled brightly. 'Now you will take me to my father, no?'

Hannibal made a face. 'We'll try. It may depend on whether Murdock can outfly a military jet with a civilian plane.'

At that moment Murdock was upside down, in the top part of a loop with the one jet fighter left. There had been three flown in from a reserve field down the coast. The first one had lost a wingtip trying to follow Murdock through a canyon and had crash-landed in the jungle. The second had used up all its ammunition and rockets without hitting anything but mountain and jungle and had returned to base to refuel. When he got back it would be too late.

One to go, Murdock thought. *Lucky I'm crazy or I wouldn't be doing these things*. 'If I had the wings of an angel!' he sang as he came out of the loop on the tail of the fighter. He went around with the jet again, almost sitting atop the plastic canopy of the fighter. The pilot chickened out and veered off, never to really recover his courage as a fighter pilot again.

Murdock serenely turned toward the San Felipe Airport. He began to sing, 'I'm coming 'round the mountain.'

Howling Mad Murdock makes a crazy landing on page 100.

From page 88.

They got out of the palace through the kitchen, where the early shift was just coming on. They were looked at curiously, but no one said anything, even when Murdock stopped to sip the guard's porridge and pronounced it 'fit for a king, jack, or ace.'

They went over a fence, along a street, and stole a car to take them to the airport. 'I'll drive,' Murdock said, ignoring Face's objections that he didn't have a licence. 'This isn't the United States. I'm not breaking the law.'

There were doubled guards on everything. They could see the Lear jet sitting by itself on the pad. There were four guards. It looked hopeless until Hannibal saw a water truck parked on a side street. It was the kind used to keep down dust, a heavy vehicle with a rack of pipe jets in front.

Ten minutes later they were breaking into a drug store in town. Twenty minutes after that the tank truck rolled up to the airport gate, driven by a dark-skinned man with a hang-dog expression and a peasant's shirt. '*Si*, I am supposed to wet down the dust,' the driver shrugged. He was waved through.

In the tank, water up to their belts, Amy, Face, and Murdock were trying to keep their balance as the water sloshed around. Spraying water, the disguised Hannibal drove the truck slowly out of sight around a hangar.

Someone jumped on the running board and a gun was stuck into Hannibal's ear. 'Hello, sucker,' B.A. said.

They peered carefully around the corner at the two guards at the entrance to Nola Frame's quarters and a lot of open corridor. Hannibal sat back and pulled Amy's ear to him, whispering a few words. She gulped, took a deep breath, and nodded.

Amy boldly walked around the corner and toward the guards. Still dressed in black, she smiled at the guards, walked past them, then stopped and turned. She started asking questions about where certain things were in the palace and definitely seemed to be flirting with one of the guards, and not the handsome one, either. He was surprised and attempted to gain her attention. Both their backs were turned toward the A-Team, and B.A. and Hannibal crept up and got them from behind.

Amy heaved a sigh of relief. 'I thought I was going to give it away by looking at you coming up behind them,' she said.

'That was a very . . . um . . . artistic performance,' Face said, and Amy blushed.

Hannibal pushed open the door and they returned to Nola's suite. They found her asleep, and Hannibal awakened her with a hand across her mouth. 'Good evening. Your rescuers have arrived.'

She blinked, then started to cry. Amy put her arm around her. 'Get out, you guys, while I get her dressed.'

Ten minutes later they were in a stolen car nearing the airport. Hannibal had been signaling with the transmitter in his cigarette lighter in the hope that Murdock was within range. It was all up to Murdock now.

B.A. gets it on page 102.

From page 53.

Hannibal fired over the heads of the two guards, and they threw themselves back into the hall. Face covered him from the roof as he climbed back up. With Amy taking Nola into her care, Hannibal and Face raced across the roof, refastened their ropes on a far wall, and went over, rappeling off the stuccoed wall of the ornate palace.

When everyone was on the ground, Face raced toward the armoured limo parked in the side lot. After the bomb in Amy's briefcase went off, the opposition scattered. It took him a few moments to hot-wire the car; by that time everyone was in and ready to go.

The ride to the airport was quick. Murdock wheeled the Lear jet onto the runway. 'San Felipe Tower, this is Escape Vehicle One requesting take-off permission.' Without pause Murdock continued. 'Thank you, San Felipe Control, this is Junior Birdman wishing you a merry chase!'

The jet lifted, and Nola looked at the inert form of B.A. Baracus lying in the aisle. 'Is he dead?'

'No,' Hannibal said. 'Just a fever.'

'The pill in the milk?' Face asked, and Hannibal shook his head.

'You know how he likes that certain kind of candy bar? I gave some to Murdock to offer B.A.' Hannibal grinned and lit up a cigar. 'I wonder how long it will take them to get the Costa Verde Air Force operational?'

'When was the last time one man took out a whole air force?' wondered Templeton Peck, looking at B.A.

END

From page 54.

They stole a jeep and piled aboard as the bomb built into Amy's secretarial briefcase went off. Alarms sounded, fire engines were heard, along with screams, shouts, and curses. Face shot out of the military parking lot as Hannibal yelled in Spanish for the guards to watch for counter-revolutionaries.

The ride to the airport was swift but uneventful. They found B.A. next to the Lear jet, which was warming up. 'Everything okay?' the burly black man asked. 'Anything for me to clean up?'

Hannibal grinned. 'Smooth as silk. I just love it when a plan comes together.'

'You're on the jazz again,' B.A. said disapprovingly. He knew Hannibal loved the excitement, the pitting of wits. 'Well, I'm off to catch the train.'

'They'll search everything,' Hannibal pointed out. 'They know who come in with us.'

B.A. glowered. 'Yeah, well, maybe I'll walk to the next country and catch a train there.'

'Without a passport? How are you getting back into the States, B.A.?'

'Hannibal,' growled B.A., balling his fists. 'You knew all this coming in, didn't you?'

'Want a pill?'

'I ain't gonna fly with that crazy Murdock. You know what he was doing while you were gone? He was reading a comic book, playing all the parts, talking like Ronald Colman and Katharine Hepburn and Marilyn Monroe and Gregory Peck!'

'B.A., I don't want you to do anything you don't want to do, but I must point out that your chances are pretty slim.'

Turn to page 96.

'Well, they're zero with Napoleon there!'

Hannibal sighed and slapped B.A. on the bare shoulder. 'Well, buddy, it was great! If you ever get back—'

'Ouch, what was that?'

'What was what?'

'That . . . on . . . my . . . shoulder . . . it . . . ' Bad Attitude Baracus rolled his eyes up and fell. Hannibal barely managed to catch the big man and keep his face from smashing on the runway.

'Face! Come help!'

'Señor, I cannot thank you enough! You have already struck a great blow for democracy in Costa Verde! The general was demoralized, word of his deal with the big corporation leaked out, and the counter-revolutionaries have struck! Costa Verde is on the way to freedom!' Nola said to Face.

'Are we on the way to dinner?' Face said softly to Nola, who smiled quietly.

'What happened?' B.A. said, coming awake.

'That's a bad fever you have, B.A.,' Hannibal said. 'I'd do something about it if I were you.'

END

From page 65.

As Hannibal climbed into the Lear jet, he saw B.A. lying peacefully in the aisle. He moved forward into the pilot's compartment as Face got the women into seats, completely filling the jet and leaving some lying on blankets.

'How'd you do it?' Hannibal said as he struggled into the co-pilot's seat.

Murdock started flipping switches and punching buttons. 'Easy as falling off a shock-treatment table, Colonel. B.A.'s been talking about taking the train back—and he knows he can't do that without papers—so I told him it had been positively inspiring to have served with him. . . . San Felipe Tower, this is IPC Special Flight requesting permission for immediate take-off . . . and offered him a beer from the executive fridge. Those pills work just fine, Colonel. He darned near killed me trying to catch him, but . . . thank you, tower, this is IPC Special Flight moving to one-three for take-off. Thank you! But I caught him and I think he's gonna be real mad at me, Colonel sir.'

'Why? He never stays really mad. It's over, it's over.'

'Well, he's big; I'm skinny; the jet door is small. . . . I think I scraped him up some.'

'I'll tell him it was his fever again.'

Murdock gunned the jet, and they started moving down the runway. 'Ooh, la, la, zee general of le air force will be a fallen soufflé when he tries to take off after us in his fighters!' Murdock said in his burlesque French accent.

'I just love it when a plan comes together,' Hannibal said with a grin.

END

From page 74.

The jeep stopped next to the plane, which Murdock was already warming up. Face and Amy hurried Nola into the sleek white jet with the phony IPC logo on the side. B.A. came running across the field, with a kind of fierce grin on his face.

'Inside!' Hannibal yelled, hoping to fake B.A. out and get him aboard, but the burly black man just grinned.

'Not this time, man! I'll take the jeep and tear out for the hills. Work with the guerrillas and—'

Blam! Pinnng! Tinkle! Blam, blam, blam!

Shots were zinging over the plane, ricocheting off the asphalt and hitting the jeep. B.A. and Hannibal threw themselves to the ground.

'You have to bring an army after you?' growled B.A.

'It's only a little banana republic army,' Hannibal protested. He raised up and emptied his clip into the night as he yelled at Murdock to get going. Then Hannibal started toward the plane, which was moving.

Hannibal tripped and sprawled on the field. A bullet tore a gash in the asphalt a foot from his face. Suddenly he was being lifted and carried in the powerful arms of B.A. Baracus, who was sprinting after the plane.

Hannibal could see Face in the door, keeping the army's collective head down by a series of blasts from an M-16. Then B.A. was pitching Hannibal through the door. A slug plunked into the door frame and B.A. threw himself inside. Face pulled on the door, swinging it up and closed to give Murdock a better aerodynamic shape.

'Go, Murdock, go!' he yelled at the top of his voice.

From page 98.

B.A., sprawled atop Hannibal, felt the plane start to lift, and he got this dazed, terrified expression on his face.

Hannibal squirmed out from under as Nola Frame asked if B.A. was shot. 'I don't think so. That's just the way he flies. C'mon, Face, let's get him into a comfortable position.'

They tugged B.A. around to lie on the floor, arranged his many chains properly, and crossed his hands over his barrel chest. Then Face sank into a seat gratefully. Costa Verde was far below, a green coastline on the blue Caribbean.

'I can't thank you enough,' Nola said, her dark eyes big.

'I'll go up forward,' Hannibal sighed, leaving Templeton Peck with the beautiful young woman.

'I'll, uh, I'll just sit back here and, uh, write up my story,' Amy said, covering a smile with her hand.

'Oh, we'll think of something,' Face said to Nola. When Amy giggled he said to her, 'Well, isn't that what you are *supposed* to say?'

'Only if you leer,' Nola said.

END

Murdock cut his engines and started dropping at once. It was a dangerous but relatively silent method. Jet planes do not do dead-stick landings like prop planes. They tend to drop more like a thrown brick.

He saw the jeep racing along the road by the field, then saw it go through into the field with the guards right after them. He was then very busy trying not to crash and missed the sudden appearance of Bad Attitude Baracus with an automatic rifle he had taken from a soldier unlucky enough to run into him.

The first shots sent the guards running, and B.A. jumped aboard the stolen jeep. The timing was almost perfect; jeep and jet arrived almost together.

"Bye, Hannibal,' B.A. said. He turned to get into the jeep, and a burst of fire from the approaching soldiers raked the vehicle. A piece of the seat back was broken off and smashed into B.A.'s forehead like a baseball bat. B.A. staggered, but he was not down.

Hannibal Smith grabbed the big black man and hustled the dazed ex-sergeant into the plane. 'No,' B.A. protested weakly, blood streaming down his face. Then he passed out. They weren't certain whether it was from the knowledge he was about to be airborne or the blow. It did, however, keep him quiet.

Hannibal grinned as father and daughter embraced. 'I love it when a plan works,' he said. 'Especially a well-paying one.'

'You don't do it for the money,' Amy accused, but Hannibal just grinned.

END

Squeezing water out of their clothes, Amy, Face, and Murdock crowded around B.A. and Hannibal. 'Four fools are out there guarding the plane,' B.A. said. 'We got about fifteen minutes before the next change of guards. What you want to do, Hannibal?' He told them.

The water truck crept up toward the plane, sprinkling down the dirt, then turned and wandered away, coming back on the runway itself. It turned and crept off around a building—where the A-Team jumped aboard on the side away from the guards—and rolled slowly along, this time on a route near the plane.

'Can't we go any faster?' B.A. complained, crouched in the passenger space.

'No, they'll get nervous.' The water truck coughed and spat, then crept on. Where the truck would block the view from the tower, it coughed, jerked, and stopped dead. Grumbling, the driver got out and opened up the hood with irritation. On the other side of the truck the A-Team dropped silently to the ground. The curious guards did have time to yell, but not to shoot. Murdock was off and running to the jet at once.

'Charge!' he yelled.

'Load up!' Hannibal ordered. With no airplanes to intercept, they got away clean.

Manuel Frame stared at the letter from his daughter. 'I am desolate . . . but . . . maybe it is not so bad, eh? Being the father-in-law of a president?'

END

B.A. led them to a storage building near the end of the runway where Murdock would stop. If he landed. If some stray bullet hadn't hit something vital. If . . .

They almost didn't hear him coming. Murdock had cut the engines and was coming down fast. It was dangerous since jets do not have the same gliding ability as prop airplanes. He lit hard and rolled to the end and deftly swung the ship around, ready for take-off.

Hannibal and the rest of the A-Team were already running. Lights were coming on in some of the airport buildings. There was a shot, then two more. A burst of machine gun fire, but it was in a different direction. Murdock dropped the hatch, then scooted back to the pilot's seat.

Hannibal fell into the co-pilot's seat. 'Go!' he commanded as he heard Face slam the hatch shut. The jet gathered speed as some soldiers ran to the edge of the runway, then scattered as Murdock swerved toward them. Moments later they were airborne.

'Where's B.A.?' Murdock asked. 'Back there?' he asked, indicating the airport.

Hannibal fired up a cigar and blew out some smoke. 'No, he's sleeping like a baby. I'll tell him it was a bullet crease on the noggin. I did cut him a touch when I slugged him with the wrench.'

'His head is as hard as a cueball, Colonel, no need to worry.'

'I'm gonna run out of ideas, though, wait and see. I'm already into brute strength and raw violence,' Hannibal said.

'And me the winner of the Pilot Safety Award for 1983,' Murdock said.

END

From page 68.

Thud! Hannibal's fist met the jaw of the guard from whom he had stopped to ask directions. Face's knotted fist thumped into the stomach of the other guard, followed by a right cross. They dragged the guards down into an alcove as Amy went into the suite.

Nola Frame stood there, trembling. 'It's all right,' Amy said soothingly. 'We've come to take you to your father.'

'Oh, thank God!' the beautiful young woman exclaimed and hugged Amy violently. 'I was so afraid!'

'Now, now, everything's fine, but we have to move, *fast!*'

The tearful girl wiped her face. 'Then I shall not need to commit the sin of suicide.' Amy's eyes blinked in surprise. 'The general, I . . . I vowed I would die first!'

'No need for that,' Hannibal said from the door. 'C'mon, let's go—*fast!*'

Guards were not placed to keep people *in* the palace, and in a few minutes they were racing toward the airport in a stolen jeep. Amy was trying to keep her expensive Beverly Hills gown clean. Face was watching their back and Hannibal was driving.

'Timing!' Face shouted over the wind. 'I *hate* it when we have to rely on close timing!'

But the Costa Verde Air Force was having a curious time trying to get its planes in the air. Oddly, even the plane flown by the man from IPC no longer seemed operational. And where *were* those guys, anyway?

The Lear jet took off smoothly, rising into the night sky on a tail of fire. Face climbed into the co-pilot's seat and buckled up. 'Well, Hannibal pulled a new one on B.A.,' Face said.

From page 104.

'The fake fever or the pill-in-the-milk?' Murdock asked.

'Neither. He acted as though he had twisted his ankle and had B.A. carry our rescued damsel aboard—after telling *her* to fake a faint. Once you started rolling ol' B.A. just froze. You know how he is. Blank-faced, staring, like a wax model of himself.'

'Poor B.A.,' Murdock said. 'We could have *so* much fun if he'd just get over his fear of flying. Why, there's nothing to it! As the late, great Satchel Paige said, 'An airline might get you killed, but it won't hurt you none.''

Face looked at Murdock. 'You think that might be calming to Sergeant Baracus?'

'No, but a comfort, maybe. Why, he and I could go fishing in Baja, swimming in Jamaica, shopping in Hong Kong. . . .' Murdock sighed. 'If I had money. Or he had money. But he puts all his into gold chains and diamond rings. Someday nine guys and a tank will mug him and he'll be broke.

'Ten guys and *two* tanks,' corrected Face.

Murdock nodded judiciously. 'Yup. You're right. Say, Face, have you ever read Kipling?' Without waiting, Murdock started reciting. The voice he used was Donald Duck's.

END

From page 78.

'Look, B.A. Maybe those guerrillas will win, maybe not. We gotta get out of here,' Hannibal said.

'Go on, git. I'm not going anywhere with that crazy Murdock. You shouldn't either. He's just as likely to fly upside down all the way to L.A. I'll go help the guerrillas, man. They can't be any worse than that general fella. I know this kinda fighting.'

'B.A., B.A., B.A.,' Hannibal said, putting his arm round Baracus, who looked suspicious. 'I'm going to miss you, Sergeant. Don't get yourself killed now. Well,' Hannibal slapped B.A. on the back, 'this is—'

'What're you doin', fool? You think you're going to stick some needle into me, man?' B.A. pulled away from Hannibal . . . and right into the needle that Face had prepared.

'Hey, you—' Blackout was swift.

'It's a good thing that stuff works quickly,' Face said. 'I'd hate to give him ten seconds or so of combat time. We'd all be shredded wheat.'

They stooped to lift him. 'Think we should carry his chains in a separate load?' Face asked.

Nola Frame looked at her father. 'Of *course*, I was a spy, father! It was for my country! But I never let him touch me, the pig!'

As Manuel Frame was making his apologies, Amy whispered to Hannibal. 'I'd hate to try and make her do something. You should see how she took care of the alarm guard! *Viva* Nola!'

END

From page 85.

'I still have it,' Murdock said proudly. 'That jet was old, but everything came back. I kinda hated to leave her. But I still got that combat sense, Colonel.'

'No one said you didn't,' Hannibal responded.

'He's still crazy, too,' B.A. growled.

'All right, everyone aboard. *Adios*, Nola.'

'Go with God, Colonel Smith. There will always be a place here for you,' she said. Ricardo Martinez had his arm around Nola and didn't look as if a return visit by such a destabilizing force as the A-Team was going to be a good idea.

'Got room for me?' B.A. asked. Hannibal, Face, and Amy stared. Murdock was in the pilot's compartment.

'You . . . want . . . to fly . . . with us?' Face asked.

'Sure, I'm over that stuff now.' He waved them in. When no one moved, he got in and they trooped along after him, quite dazed. Just as Hannibal stepped into the ship, B.A. made a grab for the door frame, ready to throw himself out. But Hannibal tripped him and slammed a needle into his shoulder, near the neck.

'*Arg*,' B.A. said and collapsed. Face and Hannibal pulled him in and shut the hatch as the Lear jet taxied for take-off.

'How'd you know?' Amy asked as they stretched B.A. out.

Turn to page 108.

'He smiled. I knew that meant only one thing.' He shrugged. 'We could have left him, I suppose, but he's my good-luck charm. And if we did, he'd *never* get back,' Hannibal said.

'And when he wakes up?' Amy asked.

Hannibal shrugged. 'He placed a bet and lost. He'll understand that.'

END

From page 79.

Manuel Frame opened the hotel door with a revolver in his hand. Without moving the barrel he gestured for Hannibal and Nola to enter, which they did, raising their hands.

'I didn't think you'd be so foolish as to come here with her,' Frame said.

'His name is Ésteban Gonzales,' Nola said. 'He betrayed my father.'

'To save my own life, Nola. Surely you can understand that,' Gonzales said.

'What I don't understand is why you wanted to rescue her,' Hannibal said. 'It can't be your conscience—betraying the father and making up for it by rescuing the daughter.'

'Hardly,' Gonzales said and smiled. 'Nola does not know it, but her father hypnotically implanted the number and identification routine of his Swiss bank account in her mind. In American dollars, it adds up to about one million nine. Her danger with the general was real, but I'm afraid nothing else was. I thought I'd have to steal her from you and—'

'Heard enough?' Hannibal said to no one in particular.

His response was explosive. Face came through the door to the adjoining suite, having picked the lock, and B.A. kicked open the door to the hall. They both had guns.

'You better get over to Switzerland and switch that money to another bank,' Face suggested to Nola.

'The money will go to help get rid of General Camarillo,' she said. 'That, and buy a few new dresses.'

END

From page 80.

Nola Frame stood on the wide windowsill with a knife at her heart. Hannibal coaxed her down carefully, explaining as well as he could that her father had sent them to rescue her.

'The general . . . he was going to . . . he . . . '

Amy put her arm around the trembling beauty as Face lifted the general's ivory-handled automatic. 'Well, we have a hostage, anyway,' he said.

'Do not be too certain of that, gentlemen,' General Camarillo said suavely. 'There are those among my staff who would take advantage of the situation and shoot me down . . . all a regrettable accident, of course . . . and you with me.'

'Well, then you better see we don't run into them, General,' Hannibal said. He took off his outer clothes, the servant livery, and tried to smooth out his rumpled businessman's suit. The others did the same.

They formed a tight little group as they exited the palace by the side door, which opened into the parking lot. A truck started up and sped up to the door. A grinning Murdock looked at them from the cab. 'Taxi?'

B.A. helped them into the back while Amy put Nola into the cab. Hannibal hefted his weapon and eyed the general, who got the picture. With the dapper officer standing at the back of the cab looking heroic, they breezed through the gate, along to the airport, and into the jet.

'Good-bye, General,' Hannibal said. 'I hope you understand why we have to tie you up like this, but we don't want a flight of jets on our trail. *Hasta la vista.*'

END

110

From page 81.

In the confusion, the A-Team raced through the palace with Hannibal shouting conflicting orders in his pay-attention-to-me voice. It didn't help that Murdock sometimes cackled like a chicken.

They broke into a number of rooms before they found a frightened Nola Frame behind a locked door, a letter opener clutched in her hand. When they told her they were there to rescue her, she broke into a bright smile. 'Even if I die, it will be on the way to freedom!' she exclaimed.

'We like to discourage that sort of talk,' Face muttered as they bustled her out. They trotted to the military parking lot. A pair of unmoving feet sticking out from behind the little guard house told them B.A. had made it that far.

They heard a truck start up, and moments later B.A. drove it up to them. 'Get in!' Hannibal ordered. He jumped into the back and told everyone to lie down on the floor. They went right out through the wire fence and were on the road to the airport in no time.

Soldiers were quick to follow, and Face, Hannibal and Murdock were using the bouncing truck as a firing platform. They were only moments ahead of the soldiers when they screeched to a halt by the jet. Murdock ran for the plane and vaulted in. B.A. took a rifle from Face and began firing at the jeeps as they pulled into the airport. Hannibal and Face got the women aboard, then looked at each other, then at B.A.'s back. 'Let's go!' Murdock bellowed.

Turn to page 112.

From page 111.

'I hate to do this,' Hannibal said. He grabbed his .45 and got behind B.A. He lifted the gun and brought it down.

'We'll tell him it's a bullet crease,' Hannibal said as they dragged the heavy man to the plane.

'Didn't we use that one on him already?' Face asked.

END

From page 50.

In the bed of the truck, Face showed Nola how to load and fire the old Garand M-1, which they had liberated. It was Nola, in fact, who put a slug through the radiator of the single pursuing jeep. They caused the airport guards to jump for their lives as the truck crashed through the striped barriers.

They drove right out on the field and to the Lear jet, which Murdock had taxied to the end of the field. By this time there were numerous vehicles after them, including a fire engine. B.A. skidded the truck to a halt and they all jumped out and into the plane except, of course, for Bad Attitude Baracus.

Hannibal caught him climbing into the cab of the truck, which was catching slugs from the distant weapons. 'Let go o' me, Hannibal,' he growled. 'You ain't trickin' me onto that plane!'

'I just wanted to shake hands, B.A., because you know we'll never see each other again.' Hannibal stuck out his hand and grinned. In his other hand, behind his back, he had a hypodermic needle of knockout juice.

But B.A. was keeping his eye on Hannibal. 'You're as crazy as Murdock! Get on that plane and—*ugh!*'

Hannibal swung the door closed on Baracus, hitting him in the head, then he jammed the needle into his arm. Seconds later B.A. was falling forward into his grasp. 'Face! Come help me!'

Templeton Peck ducked as a bullet whizzed by his ear. He helped Hannibal get B.A. into the plane. Hannibal yelled, 'Go!' the second everyone was aboard, even though his legs stuck out and the hatch was not closed. Murdock wheeled the plane around and immediately

Turn to page 114.

started his take-off. Face and Hannibal fought to get the door closed and managed only after Murdock had lifted the wheels from the runway.

Over the cabin's loudspeaker came Murdock's voice: 'This is your captain speaking, H.M. Murdock. I'll be your pilot for this trip. We will be travelling at an altitude of fifteen feet, and arrival at Los Angeles International is subject to the astuteness of the Border Patrol. Absolutely no one will be explaining the deplaning procedures in case we go down over water because it will be every man for himself. Please report all flying saucers. Have a nice flight.'

It didn't help their nerves that he ended his speech with Woody Woodpecker's bugle call.

END

B.A. drove the armoured truck noisily down the road as Hannibal told him the plan. B.A. nodded with a fierce grin, and when they got to the airport, which shared the field with the eleven planes of the Costa Verde Air Force, he swerved.

'Everybody down!' Hannibal ordered and buttoned up the flaps. He climbed up into the machine gun ring. As B.A. tore down the line, smashing wingtips, hitting tails, and, in one case, running right up over the jet fighter, Hannibal put a few well-aimed rounds into the planes on the opposite rank. One exploded and burned fiercely.

Plinnng! Whinnng! Bullets bounced off the sides of the armoured truck as B.A. wheeled it toward the Lear jet in the civilian half of the airport. Everyone but B.A. jumped out and crammed into the jet. Then Hannibal jumped out as the jet started to move slowly off.

'I'm staying here with you, B.A.!' he shouted.

'You're crazy, Colonel! We'll get killed!'

'Then we'll die together, old friend!'

'Colonel, I can't let you do this, I—'

Hannibal staggered, shouted out a cry of pain, and fell to the ground. Without a moment's hesitation B.A. jumped out, scooped him up, and trotted toward the taxi-ing jet. He shoved Hannibal in, but his legs kept falling out and no one was helping from the inside. Growling, B.A. climbed aboard and pulled Hannibal in, then shut the door. Then he went catatonic.

The moment B.A. stopped moving, Hannibal sat up and dusted himself off. 'Home, James,' he shouted to Murdock.

END